# Clausdrum
# (Life without Parole)

# Table of Contents

# Chapter 1
# My New Home

As the guards escorted me down the corridor to my cell, all I could focus on was the horrible stench in the air. It was a combination of the smell of mildew and sweat. For the past week, as I sat in solitary confinement with only my thoughts to entertain me, I knew this day would come. As much as I dreaded it, I knew I would have to face it sooner or later. I was being escorted to the small eight by nine cell that would be my home for the next sixty years or more.

The guards towered over me in size, of course. They were both men that stood about six feet tall and I am small in size even compared to other women. I'm about five feet two inches and thin built. I'm not very strong physically but I can take care of myself rather well. The yellow jump suit I was given to wear was slightly too large for my frame and the shoes they gave me had no laces. Apparently, no shoes laces was one of the many unwritten rules that dated back for more than one hundred years.

The chains on my hands and feet were clanging loudly against the metal walkway that I was being escorted on. The guards were extremely unfriendly and didn't make eye contact.

They acted as if I weren't really human. The one guard to my left gave me a shove and said, "Move a little faster. We ain't got all day". I stumbled slightly, almost tripping over the shackles and tried to walk faster. These guards were not to be challenged and I had learned that early on during my stay here. I was disciplined on my first night.

I had just arrived and was told that I would be in solitary confinement for the first week of my stay. Apparently, this was protocol for the prison. Everyone spends their first week in solitary and some have even spent longer than that. They told me that the purpose was to acquaint me with their rules and regulations and to learn my place in this prison prior to being released into the general population.

When they took me to that section of the building and walked me to my isolated cell, the guard shoved me, almost knocking me down. I turned around and spit in his face. I received a beating like no other I had ever received. My right eye was swollen shut for two days and I could taste my own blood for hours after the door was slammed shut and I was left alone to think about what had just occurred. In that moment, I learned that the prisoners at Clausdrum have no rights.

Later that night after dinner trays had been served through the small window in the door, I was sitting alone in the quiet of solitaire when the slit of my door slid open and a pamphlet was dropped onto the ground through the opening. A voice from the other side of the door said, "Here's your new holy bible. Study it. Breathe it. Smell it. Taste it. Know it. This is the book of rules and regulations that will apply to you from this day forward and until you die in the rotting hell hole you now call home." I didn't move from my corner of the tiny closed-in cell until about five minutes after the small window in the door slammed shut again and I knew the person was gone.

I inched my way over to the front of the cell to pick up the brochure. My body was still aching from the beating I had received

5

from the welcoming committee. I swallowed yet another small amount of blood, picked up the pamphlet and crawled back over to the corner that had a small light overhead. The pamphlet wasn't very large and opened up to three sections.

The first section contained the rules and regulations that prisoners are to abide by. The second section was a list of the daily routines and a schedule that seemed extremely rigid. The third section was a list of violations and the punishments that accompanied each one. I began reading the first section, which was titled 'The Ten Commandments'.

1.      All prisoners will obey the guards and their superiors without questioning or arguing with their authority.

2.      Prisoners will not be permitted to participate in any activities, free time or rest periods without receiving permission from the authorities beforehand unless it is scheduled.

3.      If a particular job is assigned to any prisoner, that prisoner will perform that job until the supervisor of that job deems the job completed as instructed.

4.      Prisoners will have limited time to interact with one another and will obey their superiors when instructed to cease communications with another prisoner.

5.      Prisoners will keep their cells neat and clean at all times with no obstruction in the view of any area of that cell.

6.      Prisoners will follow the schedule that has been assigned to them and will not veer from that schedule in any way.

7.      No smoking is allowed inside the prison at any time. Prisoners will only be allowed to use the designated areas in the courtyard for smoking.

8.      No prisoner will be allowed to make trades with one another in any form. Prisoners will receive credits for work performed that can be used to purchase items in the prison store.

9.      All needed supplies will be provided to prisoners and no alterations are to be made to the supplies provided.

10.     All prisoners must be neat and clean at all times. Showers are not a privilege but a requirement and all prisoners will be expected to use the shower each day.

"Home sweet home" I said to myself as I turned the page to look over the schedule. According to this little pamphlet I held in my hands, my life was going to be a constant boot camp from this day forward. The schedule was rigid and had activities listed for every minute of the day. It didn't seem to allow much time for boredom. We were to wake at six o'clock each morning and seven on the weekends.

We were to clean our cells, make our beds and be facing outward at our prison doors within fifteen minutes of waking. From there, we line up to go to the cafeteria for breakfast. After breakfast, work is done in shifts. The morning shift reports to their assigned places by seven thirty and the rest of the prisoners are herded to the courtyard for free time.

After lunch, the two shifts change and those who had spent the morning in the courtyard arrive at their designated jobs by one o'clock. The prisoners who had performed morning work are now allowed to go to the courtyard. After dinner, we are lined up once again to take showers. By seven o'clock in the evening we are to be back in our cells and lights go out at nine.

It seemed very straight forward and easy to remember. As long as I could remain invisible to the guards, I felt I had nothing to worry about. I glanced over the third section, which contained violations and consequences. There were several violations that were categorized as severe and each one landed a prisoner in solitary confinement. The duration of the punishment depended solely on the violation committed.

1.    Fighting among prisoners is unacceptable and will result in serving time in solitary confinement for up to one week.
2.    Failure to show up at an assigned area on time will result in solitary confinement for one hour for every minute late to the assigned area.
3.    Refusing to obey an authority figure will result in solitary confinement for the duration that the said authority figure deems

necessary.

4.     Disobeying or disrespecting any authority will result in being sent to solitary confinement for the remainder of that day without the privilege of remaining meals for that day.

5.     Disorderly conduct or uncleanliness is not allowed and will result in solitary confinement until the prisoner is willing to behave and follow instructions as stated in the rules and regulations.

For the remainder of the time I spent in solitary, I looked over the pamphlet a few more times, ate my three meals each day and thought about the rest of my life in this horrible place. As many times as I looked over that pamphlet, I never did see anything written about the rights of the prisoner's or of the fact that a beating apparently precedes time spent in solitary confinement. The more I let this information sink in, the more afraid I became about my future here.

As we continued down the corridor, I had a little trouble seeing my way. It was approximately eleven thirty at night and lights out had occurred hours ago. There was a small amount of light along the hallways that slightly illuminated the way and as we turned the corner to the main cell area where I would be assigned a cell, I studied the surroundings the best I could.

The cell area was a large open floor plan with two levels and a staircase that went up on both sides to each level. There were three rows of cells and they were all organized by letter. The very first area from the direction I was being escorted from was Cell Block C, the row next to that was Cell Block B and the row that I was to occupy on the first level was called Cell Block A. Along both sides of the prison area, there were approximately fifty cells on each level. Each one contained a bed, a toilet with no privacy and a fold out table and chair. There was also a single bar nailed to the back wall of each prison cell that had clean yellow jumpsuits hanging up and shoes sitting neatly on the floor just below it.

To the very back of the open floor plan, there was a balcony that was on the upper level with a lighted office area just behind that. As we moved toward my cell, I noticed that there were two guards standing in the balcony area looking over at all the cells. I suppose they were the night shift guards that were to watch the prisoners sleep at night and to make sure there was no suspicious activity. I couldn't help but wonder to myself what type of activity could possibly exist in a lock down type of prison such as this one but I guess they couldn't be too careful. After all, this is a maximum security prison that houses societies most dangerous monsters.

My cell was on the right hand side from the entrance and as we walked over toward the area that I would occupy, the guard gave me another shove. This time, I felt that he was just exerting his authority over me for his own narcissistic pleasure. It took everything I had to not shove him back despite the shackles but I refrained as soon as I felt the throbbing in my cheek bone where the bruises were healing from my last beating. I continued to walk toward my cell.

As soon as we were in front of the cell, the guard to my right swiped his key card and the cage opened up. It was just like all the other cells, not that I expected anything else. My bed was neatly made with one fleece blanket and a sheet, corners tucked tightly. The fold out table was up against the wall and the chair was in the left hand corner of the cell. One of the guards gave me a hard shove from the back, almost knocking me over as I stumbled into my new home.

I turned around and held up my cuffed hands without saying a word and another guard came over with a key to release my restraints. As I stood there, I heard a couple of the other inmates shuffling and mumbling to themselves. The loud clanging of my heavy chains must have awakened a couple of the others. I heard a voice from across the hall, "What's all the noise?" One of the guards from the balcony replied immediately in a loud voice, "Hey! Quiet down there! You know the rules. No talking after lights out."

9

Once the chains were off, the guards left me standing there in my cell as the doors to my cage slammed shut. Before walking away, one of the guards looked at me and said, "Welcome to Clausdrum, your new home for the rest of your pathetic life." I replied with a slight amount of sarcasm to my voice, "Thanks. Glad to be here." As soon as I had said this, I wished that I could have taken it back as the guard slammed his night stick against the metal bars. I found myself jump slightly and cower. I guess that beating was still fresh in my mind and now I knew that this guard would be watching me more closely for a while.

I stood there for a few moments after they had walked away before I began looking around at my new cell. I noticed right away that there was a set of pajamas folded neatly on the bed. Although they didn't look very comfortable, I knew they had to be more comfortable than the yellow jump suit I was currently wearing.

I also noticed that there were three more clean yellow jump suits hanging on the bar in the very back corner of my cell. I slipped out of my jumpsuit and changed into the pajamas. There were two empty baskets next to the desk. Both were clearly labeled. One had the word laundry written on the side of it and the other had the word waste. I put the jump suit into the laundry basket and settled into my new bed.

As I lay there staring up at the ceiling, I couldn't get to sleep. All I could do was think back to my last day of freedom. It was well over a month ago when I was taken in and put on trial. During the duration of the trial, I was held in a jail with much less security and strict rules. The guards in the jail were friendly and laid back compared to the guards at Clausdrum. We had more freedom and there wasn't a strict schedule like there was in this place. They allowed for more free time and the cells were more open like cubicles rather than individual cages.

Still, I'll never forget that last day of fresh air and freedom. It was a Tuesday afternoon at the end of September. The weather was perfect, not too hot or too cold. The leaves were just beginning

10

to change as autumn was approaching. I had just gotten back to my home town after being gone for quite some time. I had gone straight to an old friend's house a few blocks from where I had grown up. It wasn't the nicest area in town.

My friend wasn't rich by any means and neither was I. But, it was the life we knew and grew up in. We sat out on her front porch, drank a couple of beers and watched the kids run around and play. I couldn't have asked for a better day.

As we sat there talking, she hushed me and the kids. "Shhh! Did you hear that?" I listened closely as we all stayed as quiet as we could. At first I didn't hear it but then the sound of a low humming reached my ears. "I hear it. Mini Sirens. I wonder who they could be after." I said to my friend. She smiled and replied, "In this neighborhood, they could be after anyone." This was true. The neighborhood didn't house the best of people in our society and, from time to time, the Mini Sirens would pay a visit on someone with an outstanding warrant on their arrest. It was rather common seeing them during my childhood.

Mini Sirens had been around for as long as I could remember. The government had created these devises many years ago, well before I was ever born. They are actually called AK759s but the layman's term has always been Mini Sirens. They are small blue computerized saucers that can hone in and keep tract of a certain person until the police arrive and shut them down. Each person has a small microchip installed just under the skin when they are born. This little chip contains every detail of that person including birthday, certain aspects of their DNA, along with an ID number that is assigned to each person upon birth.

The Mini Sirens, along with the microchips assigned to each person, have been extremely beneficial in many ways. For one, there are fewer criminals in the streets. However, this has caused a problem with overcrowded prisons. On the other hand, the police no longer have to chase someone through alleys and buildings with the chance of losing sight of that person.

11

When hunting down a criminal, the police just input the person's information into the Mini Sirens. The Mini Sirens then tract down that person by matching the information the police entered with the information in the microchip that each person has implanted under their skin. No person has ever been successful at losing the Mini Sirens once they are honed in on them. As the Mini Sirens remain locked in to that person, the police would track the Mini Sirens. Therefore, they would know exactly where the criminal was located.

The microchip also acted as a type of tracking devise so that parents would always know where their children were. Children were no longer abducted, and if they were, it wouldn't be long afterward that they were found. The personal information from the microchip would simply be plugged into a laptop and the laptop would provide a map that could allow the parents to track the exact location of the lost child.

We all remained quiet as we heard the Mini Sirens getting louder. We held our breath as we anticipated the site of them coming after someone and getting excited about watching that person attempt to lose these little devises. It wasn't the best entertainment but it was the only entertainment we got in a place like this. Suddenly, one of the kids yelled as he pointed upward, "I see them!" We all looked in that direction and sure enough there were three of them moving through the air toward the place we were standing.

As I stood there watching them come closer and closer, my heart sank as I realized they were heading toward me. My friend looked at me and said, "Roxy? Where did you say you were all this time? What did you do?" I didn't know what to say. I panicked and then I ran. I dropped my beer on the ground and took off around the trailer and toward the chain length fence. I didn't realize I could run as fast as I ran that day but I suppose I was charged by my own adrenaline as I feared the worse. I hopped over the fence and ran into the wooded area directly behind my friend's neighborhood.

I knew the area well since I had grown up on this side of town. I realized that knowing my way around wasn't going to help me but I couldn't stop my legs from moving as fast as they did. I was sweating as I continued to dodge trees and bushes. I ran until I came to another opening on the other side of the wooded area. I ran out into the street and quickly turned straight down an alley.

I briefly looked over my shoulder to see if the Mini Sirens were still tracking me. At first, there was nothing. I didn't see them or hear them. Then, the three saucers turned the corner and were moving just as fast as I was.

I saw a door that was slightly open in the alley. I rushed through it and found myself in some sort of abandoned warehouse. I kept running. I ran all the way to the other side of the warehouse and went through another doorway, which led me to yet another alley. I turned left and continued running. The Sirens came down from above the building and focused back on me again. They had gone over the building that I had just gone through.

As I ran straight to the end of the alley, I was met on the other side by a police barricade. They had been tracking the devises and knew where I would end up. The chase was over. One of the officers said, "Roxanne Beatry? You're under arrest for the murder of Wesley Strand." I could feel my heart beating hard in my chest as I struggled to catch my breath. I was told to put my hands on my head and another police officer came behind me and put the handcuffs on. It was over.

As I lay there in my bed that night thinking about the last moments of my past life, I dreaded what was to come in my new life. I had already angered two guards and knew that flying under the radar was just not possible. All I could do was try my hardest to control my anger and try to follow the rules the best I could. This was going to be my home for the rest of my life. October 31, 2070 was my first day as a prisoner at the most infamous maximum security prison for women in the world.

# Chapter 2
# My First Day

I was awakened without warning by a loud whistle blowing throughout the prison area. As I scrambled to get out of bed, I could hear the other women scrambling around in their cells as well. I tried to focus on what was happening as I struggled to wake up completely. I remembered the schedule they had given me to study. As I looked out toward the other cells, I saw that the other women were moving quickly around their own cells as they made their beds, wiped down their folding tables, placed them against the wall and got dressed as quickly as they could. I realized I had to move fast.

I pulled my covers up over the bed, tucking the corners tightly just the way I had found it the previous night. I took off my pajamas and grabbed a yellow jump suit from the hanger. After getting dressed, I folded my pajamas and placed them neatly on the bed. As soon as I was finished, I heard someone from across the way, "Hey, new girl." I looked to see another prisoner trying to discretely get my attention. As soon as she realized she had my attention, she continued, "Don't fold your pajamas. They give you a new set each day. Put the pajamas in the basket."

Just then, a guard came walking down toward my cell. She

14

seemed suspicious as she came closer and heard the other inmate talking to me. I quickly grabbed the pajamas off the bed and threw them into the basket and faced outward toward the prison bars as I remembered seeing in the pamphlet. As I stood there, I could see the other prison cells much clearer than I could the previous night. I saw that the other women were quickly getting into position just as I was, facing outward toward the bars. The prison guard walked past me and glared as she held up her night stick as a warning for me to not speak during clean up.

Then, a guard from the balcony blew the whistle again. We all stood as still as we possibly could as a couple of the guards walked from cell to cell checking for cleanliness and doing a head count. The guards that were doing the physical check of our cells each had a computer tablet. Each time they would walk past a cell and confirm that the prisoner was present and the cell was clean, they would type something into their tablets.

I couldn't see the other cell blocks from my prison cell, but I assumed that the same thing was occurring in those areas as well. I wondered to myself what they were typing and I wondered what they would do if someone was missing or not standing where they should be. After seeing how strict these guards were, I hoped to never find out.

Once it was confirmed that every cell was cleaned and every prisoner was present, the whistle blew again. This time the doors to all of our cells opened at once. It was now time to line up for breakfast. As soon as I realized this, my stomach rumbled with hunger. The whistle blew again and this time the guard in the balcony yelled for us to form two straight lines on either side. With two levels, it was actually four lines but I wasn't about to argue.

Once we all stood outside of our cells facing toward the exit of the cell area, we were instructed to being walking toward the cafeteria. The guards herded us very well as the lines from the upper areas combined with the lower areas, eventually becoming two lines toward the cafeteria. We walked out of the cell area and down a smaller corridor.

Once we entered the cafeteria, we continued in two lines and split off in opposite directions. The cafeteria had two food stations on both sides with tables lined up in the middle of the two lines. I was on the right.

I did exactly what the person in front of me did. I grabbed a tray at the beginning of the food line, and held out my tray at each station while a woman working behind the counter put food on my tray. I didn't complain or even open my mouth to say a single word. I was too scared. The first woman put a plate of scrambled eggs on my tray. The second woman gave me a small bowl of over ripe fruit. The last woman at the food station gave me one slice of toast with no butter and a glass of water.

I definitely felt that I had reason to complain about this meal but I continued through the line without speaking. I knew that I had no right to complain. This was prison and I had to get used to it. This was going to be what I would eat every day for the rest of my life. However, I couldn't help but secretly crave waffles and pancakes with real eggs and syrup.

Once my tray was full of all the food I would get for breakfast, I turned toward the tables to find a place to sit down. The woman in front of me had already disappeared into the crowd so I wasn't sure where I should go. I spotted a place in the corner where no one was sitting yet. I started over toward that way. As I was walking, I heard a voice from behind me saying, "Hey, new girl. I wouldn't go over that way if I were you. Follow me. You can sit with me over here."

It was the same woman who had warned me earlier about putting my pajamas in the laundry rather than folding them and putting them back on my bed. I turned and followed her to a table that was on the opposite side of the cafeteria. She was a middle-aged, heavy set woman and much taller than me. She had blonde hair that was shoulder length and probably hadn't been brushed in quite a while. She had a look of intimidation in her mannerisms but I trusted her already.

Once we were seated at the table, she instructed me to put my hands to my side and not touch the tray. I did just as she said and she did the same thing. I then noticed, as people were settling in to a place to sit, they were also putting their hands to their sides. Once the commotion died down and everyone was seated, the whistle blew again. Everyone began eating their stale breakfast immediately and so did I.

"My name's Jaye. You got a name other than new girl?" She said in between shoveling food into her mouth. I replied, "Name's Roxy. You seem to know your way around. How long have you been here?" She stopped eating for a moment and smiled, "Too long. Ten years and counting." I couldn't even imagine being in this place for ten years even though I knew it was inevitable that I would one day be saying the same thing.

Once we were done with breakfast, the whistle blew again and everyone began taking their trays to the back of the cafeteria where there was a disposal rack for clean-up. Once I had dropped off my tray, I panicked. Everyone was lining up either at the back of the cafeteria by the doors that led to the courtyard or they were leaving the cafeteria through the front entrance to go to their jobs. I didn't know where I was supposed to go. No one had assigned a job for me or a schedule. I turned around to find Jaye but she was gone.

As I stood there wondering what to do next, a telegraphic hovercraft floated over the crowd of prisoners and stopped directly in front of me. The screen opened up and the words, 'A message from the Warden' appeared on the screen. After a few seconds, the words disappeared and the Warden himself showed up on the screen with a pre-recorded message for me.

As he stared straight ahead, he stated, "Roxanne Beatry, your schedule is as follows: You will be assigned to the courtyard

17

for the first half of the day and then you will report to laundry duty after lunch. You will be at your job no later than one o'clock pm and you will report to Officer Yander in the prison area in front of Cell Blocks A, B and C. Officer Yander will give you instructions on your job at that time. Thank you." the screen shut back down and the telegraphic hovercraft flew back over the crowd of prisoners and out of the cafeteria.

I was relieved that I wouldn't have to report to a job first thing after breakfast. I headed to the line by the door to go to the courtyard. I really didn't know what to expect once I got to the courtyard but I figured I would be able to blend in and not make waves with anyone.

Once we were lined up at the backdoor, the guard standing at the very front of the line began reinforcing the rules to us. "Once you are outside, there will be no fighting, arguing, or disrespecting others in any way. Do I make myself clear?" Several of the prisoners yelled back, "Yes, Sir!" I remained quiet and stood as still as I could in the line.

The doors opened and we began filing outside into the fresh air. The courtyard was a large fenced in area with picnic tables to the right, a basketball court in the middle and a track that circled the entire yard. In the distance on the far side of the basketball court, there were metal bleachers. I wasn't sure where to go so I wandered slowly toward one of the picnic tables to sit down. Everyone else seemed to know exactly where their place was in the courtyard.

A few of the women congregated in the basketball court while others wandered over to the edge of the courtyard and stood along the fence line. As I got closer to the picnic tables, they began filling up quickly with different groups of women. I started to wonder if it would be a bad idea for me to try and sit with one of the tight nit groups. I walked even slower as I tried desperately to brainstorm on where I should go.

To my relief, Jaye came walking up beside me and said, "I wouldn't sit there either. Come with me." She turned toward the bleachers and I followed after her. Once we were at the bleachers she picked a spot in the middle and sat down. I sat down next to her and studied my new surroundings.

"Do you know why I picked this spot?" Jaye said to me in a hushed tone. I shook my head. She discretely pointed to the building and said, "Look up there. Do you see those small black boxes with the red lights flashing?" I did see them. They were mounted on the wall along the building and continued along the fence behind us. There were also a couple of them mounted on top of the basketball hoops.

I had never seen anything like it before and had no idea what they were. Jaye continued to explain, "Those are called Recorder Spies. They can pick up everything we say and transmit it live to those guards standing up in that tower over there." I looked to my left and saw the tower that overlooked the courtyard. There were a couple of people inside moving around. I asked, "So, they are listening to us talk right now?"

"Not exactly. Notice how each one of the recorder spies are spaced apart by twenty feet. Each one can pick up sounds within ten feet so each of them should be twenty feet away from the other." This made sense to me and I nodded to let Jaye know that I understood. She continued, "The two Recorder Spies behind us are not exactly spaced like the others. They are spaced twenty five feet away from each other. It's only these two that are slightly off from the rest. So, if we sit directly in between them and talk quietly, they can't hear us."

I laughed, "Jaye, you have had way too much time on your hands in this place." She laughed as well and then put her finger to her mouth as a signal for me to quiet my voice. "Have you actually proven your theory on this?" I inquired. "Actually, no. Let's give it a try." Jaye lowered her voice and leaned toward me as she said, "Officer Lang is a jack-ass." I looked at her in disbelief as I

19

chuckled a little at her statement. She leaned back and added, "If I'm still here by this evening and not in solitary, then we'll know it worked."

We sat there for a few moments enjoying the fresh air when Jaye pointed to a group of women standing by the basketball hoops. She explained, "See those women there? Don't go near them. They're always looking for a fight, especially with new people. The two women in the front were big into drug trafficking." I was surprised and said, "Drug Trafficking? So, they got busted for drugs?" Jaye said, "Not exactly. They got busted for murder. Drug related, of course, but by the time the police caught up with them, they had killed seventeen people combined."

"Those women over at the tables to the left are nice enough but they're the lesbian group. If you interact with them, they'll assume you're one too. Next thing you know, your somebodies bitch in this place." I made a mental note to myself to avoid that group in order to minimize any confusion. Jaye continued to point out a few other congregated groups in the courtyard and gave me reasons to avoid each one.

She pointed toward another group of women who were standing by the fence as she explained, "That group over there are the gossipers. If you want everyone to know your business, talk to them. I guarantee that every person in this place will know by the end of the day. They spread news like wildfire. They're harmless otherwise. However, I've heard that they've been known to make things up just to stir trouble. So, my advice is to not get on their bad side."

Once Jaye had pointed to every group I could see, I noticed that there was one person Jaye hadn't pointed out. She was sitting by herself on the ground, rocking back and forth and mumbling to herself. I pointed toward her and asked, "What about her? What's her story?" Jaye looked over in that direction and replied, "Oh, you mean Crazy Chris? She's nuts. No one talks to her and she doesn't talk to anyone else except for herself. I don't know. Maybe she has imaginary friends or something."

"Maybe she's lonely" I said quietly as I studied her movements. She was a small girl about my age. She was probably a little taller than me by a few inches but she was thin with long brown hair that was in knots. She had a bit of a crazed look in her big blue eyes as she stared straight ahead. Jaye chuckled as she continued, "Lonely? No she's not lonely. She's crazy. She's been here since she was eighteen years old for the murder of her parents. Story has it, she hacked them up one night with an ax." I had a hard time believing that someone as innocent looking as Crazy Chris could have possibly been accused of such a horrific crime.

Jaye could see the disbelief on my face. "It was a cut and dry case. Rumor has it, the neighbors had heard screaming coming from the house and called the police. She had killed her father first while he slept. One whack to the head and he was gone. The mother apparently woke up to see what Chris had done and fled. Crazy Chris went after her. She got her good in the arm with the ax on the way out of the house from the back door. Then, she finished her off in the wooded area directly behind the house. Crazy Chris was covered in blood and both her parents were dead by the time the police arrived on the scene. As far as I know, she's been mumbling to herself like that ever since."

We sat there in quiet for a few moments before I asked, "What about you? Why are you here?" Jaye suddenly looked uncomfortable by my question and I realized I probably shouldn't have been so abrupt with asking. She answered anyway. "I've been here for ten years and I'm almost fifty years old." I wasn't sure where she was going with this but I let her continue.

"I had a normal life outside of this place. I was married and had one child. She's grown now, of course and occasionally writes me a letter. But, there was one thing I hadn't told anyone for many years. My husband used to beat me and always made me feel stupid. The entire time we were married, I thought about getting a divorce but then my daughter would grow up without a normal

21

family. I waited until she was grown and moved out on her own before I voiced this to my husband. When I told him I wanted a divorce, he beat me so bad I couldn't see straight. That night, while he was sleeping, I took the shot gun out of the closet and quietly went into the bedroom. I shot him dead while he slept."

As I sat there and took the information in, I realized I would have done the same thing in that situation. The more I thought about it, the more surprised I was by the fact that she had gotten a life sentence in a place like this. She was abused and trapped. I commented, "Why did you get sent here? That's not a horrible crime. I'm surprised a jury didn't have more sympathy than that."

Jaye shook her head as she said, "The jury felt that my crime was premeditated. Plus, when the lawyer asked me if I had any regrets about it, I said that I didn't and given the chance I would have done it again." At that moment, I sympathized with Jaye because she wasn't the only one who didn't regret the crime they committed. I knew that I would have committed my crime again if given the chance as well. I then wondered how many of these other women would commit their crime again if given the chance.

We sat outside and continued with small talk for a little while before the whistle blew once again. I mumbled as we stood up, "I'm going to shove that whistle somewhere." Jaye heard my comment and reassured me, "Don't worry, you get used to it after a while." I had to trust that I would because I was already tired of hearing the piercing sound before and after every activity.

We lined up again at the door that led into the cafeteria and began filing in for lunch. Once we were inside, I saw that the women who had worked during the morning hours were already in line getting food. I filed in behind one of the lines and grabbed a tray. I was given a tuna fish sandwich with a small salad that consisted of wilted ice berg lettuce and a small tomato. Water was served as the beverage.

Jaye was right behind me and we walked over to the same table we had sat at earlier for breakfast. I instinctively picked up my sandwich but Jaye grabbed my arm as a reminder that we were supposed to wait until we're told to start eating. I sat there with my hands at my side until the whistle blew again. Everyone began eating. As I ate my stale sandwich, I reminded myself that I had to get used to this way of life. After all, this was my life now and I had no choice but to make the best of it.

# Chapter 3
# Laundry Duty

After disposing my tray onto the conveyor belt I turned toward the front entrance of the cafeteria and headed out to the cell blocks to meet with Officer Yander. I was nervous just thinking about the type of work I would have to do and who I would be working with. After talking with Jaye about some of the other inmates, I didn't know what to expect.

As I turned the corner to go toward Cell Block A, I heard someone calling out to me. I turned and saw an officer standing in the row of Cell Block B along with three other prisoners. It was approximately five minutes until one o'clock so I was early for my first day.

I walked over to meet up with them and the officer introduced himself as Officer Yander. He had a tablet and was typing something into it while he explained what we were going to do, "Now that we're all here, I'm going to take you all downstairs to the laundry area where you will be folding clothes and distributing them to the correct bins."

We then followed him as he led us back toward the cafeteria and down a stairway that was to the right of the doors that led out to the courtyard. Once we were in the lower level of the building, we walked down a long corridor and into an area that had washers and dryers. There were already women in this area that were moving clothes from the washers to the dryers and then putting them into large bins. Officer Yander instructed us to each grab one of the large bins at the end of the room and follow him down another corridor that led to a room to the left of the showers.

The room he led us to was large with a counter at the front and small bins lining the other three walls. There were hundreds of small bins and each one of them was labeled with a prisoner's number. I understood right away that we were expected to fold every piece of clothing and place them into the correct bin, matching the numbers on the clothing to the numbers on the bins.

Each of us had a bin that was full to the rim with unfolded uniforms and pajamas. The pajamas were also jumpsuits except that they were made of a softer material and were dark gray. They each had numbers on them just like the yellow jumpsuits we were all wearing. Officer Yander explained what we were to do, even though I already had understood from the site of the room and the clothing in the bins. However, this confirmed that my assumption was correct.

As we all took a piece of clothing from our bins, Officer Yander grabbed a chair and sat down at the entrance to the room. I wondered to myself if we would ever be able to fold every piece of clothing and match them up before dinner. It was overwhelming to think that we would even make a dent in these laundry bins.

The other three women didn't talk much. They just diligently folded clothing and placed them in the bins. I recognized one of the women right away from the courtyard. She was one of the women from the group Jaye had pointed out near the basketball court. This was the group that picked fights according to Jaye. As I watched her fold clothes from the corner of my eye, she seemed rather harmless to me.

Another woman that was assigned to this duty was from the gossipers group. Jaye had said that they were harmless unless you give them a reason to spread lies about you. Otherwise, they don't bother anyone much. The third woman that was folding clothes with me didn't look familiar at all. I didn't remember seeing her in the courtyard but there were a lot of prisoners and she could have been sitting at the picnic tables.

As I continued to work diligently, the woman from the drug dealers group moved closer to me and began taking clothes from my bin. I wasn't about to complain at first but then she leaned in and discretely said, "I'm watching you, new girl." I didn't really know how to respond to that so I said, "You and every guard in this place." She looked up from the bin and replied, "Are you really going to give me a reason to kick your ass?"

Just then, the prison guard looked up and yelled, "Hey! No talking! Get back to work." She moved back over to her bin and continued folding clothes. I did the same and for the rest of the afternoon, we worked in silence. She gave me a threatening look every now and then but I tried my best to ignore it. I didn't need any trouble on my first day. Eventually, Officer Yander instructed us to stop folding and to return our bins to the washer and dryer area of the prison. We followed him down the corridor, placed our bins against the back wall and continued up the stairs and toward the cafeteria for dinner.

Once we were in the cafeteria line, I looked around for Jaye but didn't see her. I moved through the line with my tray and then walked over toward the table that Jaye and I had been sitting at together for each meal. Once I was seated, I was relieved to see Jaye walking over to the table with her tray. I definitely did not want to be caught alone in this place. After being threatened during my work, I was beginning to realize that the prison guards were the least of my worries.

After the whistle blew and we began eating, I quietly said, "One of the girls from the drug group threatened me." Jaye stopped

26

eating and stared at me for a moment before replying, "Once you've been targeted by one of them, it's over. You're gonna get your ass kicked. You just don't know when or where it's going to happen." My heart sank at that news. I couldn't believe that I had made an enemy on my first day and didn't even do anything to bring it on.

Jaye continued to scarf down her dinner but stopped for a moment to say, "Don't worry, I got your back. I'll try to look out for you, kid." I felt a little better knowing that I had at least one friend here that would stick out her neck for me. Then I wondered what job Jaye had to do each day and what type of people she had to spend the afternoon with. I asked, "What job are you assigned to?"

"Well, I used to have laundry duty like you, but for the past year I've been assigned to the hospital. I'm the Nurses Aid. They promoted me to that since I don't cause trouble and I stay away from everyone else here. No one has ever threatened me and I don't bother them. I guess they're too scared of my size." I found myself wishing that I was six feet tall and overweight like Jaye.

After we had finished our dinner and disposed of our trays, we were told to sit back down and wait for our table to be called to the shower area. Apparently, a few tables at a time were called to head down for showers and each group has five minutes to get washed up. Jaye and I were one of the first to be called.

Along with about twenty five other women, we were led out of the cafeteria and down the same set of stairs I had gone down for laundry duty. We walked past the washers and dryers and down the same corridor as before. But this time we walked straight ahead to the very end of the hall which opened up to a shower area. It was a long room with short cubicles and thirty shower heads along the wall. They were all turned on and we were to get undressed along some benches in front of the actual showers.

There were a couple of large bins where we were to put our

27

clothing and a guard that stood next to it that handed us each a bar of soap. The soap I received looked as if it had been used before. I didn't complain since I knew it wouldn't do me any good. I took my soap and found a shower head to stand under.

After getting cleaned up, I followed the crowd to the right where there was another guard standing in front of a doorway to the room I had been folding clothes in earlier. As we walked up to the guard, she handed us each a towel and instructed us to throw our bar of soap into a bin next to her. I realized at that moment that my soap had been used before. I cringed at the thought of who had used it before me.

As we wrapped our towels around ourselves and headed into the room with clean clothes, I noticed that the guards were already filing a new group of women in for their showers. They had a system to this that seemed to work as they moved us all along like cattle.

Once I was in front of the counter in the clothing room, the guard behind the counter told me to raise my left arm. I did and she pointed a scanner toward the area where my microchip was located. It lit up and she called out my prison number to another guard who was standing near the bins. He searched the bins for my number and took the clothing from the bin and handed it to her.

It was only a pair of pajamas and clean undergarments. Some of the prisoners had gotten pajamas, undergarments and a clean yellow jumpsuit. I still had two more in my cell that hadn't been worn yet. I figured that I'd get new ones by the time I needed them.

After I had my new clothes, I was herded through yet another door and over to another room that had benches lined up alongside one another. There were already several women in the room that had removed their towels and were getting dressed into their pajamas. I found an empty spot on one of the benches and did the same.

We had taken our shoes off prior to entering the shower area, so once we were dressed we had to move back out to the corridor and locate our shoes. They also had our prison numbers labeled on the side of each shoe so it wasn't too difficult to locate my shoes out of the thirty pairs that were originally lined up against the wall. I bent down to pick up my shoes and felt someone shove me as they walked by.

I then heard a familiar voice, "Watch where your walking, new girl." It was the woman from the drug group that had threatened me earlier. She seemed to really have it out for me. I was scared but tried my best not to show it.

I ignored her comment, put on my shoes and followed my group out toward the cell area once again. Since my group had gone first, we arrived in our cells well before we were required to be there. The guards didn't seem to care that we were locked up too early. They continued to herd us to our cells and as I walked into mine, a guard slammed the cage shut behind me.

I noticed that some of the women had pulled their tables down and were either reading or writing in order to pass time. I had nothing to do. I was already in my pajamas and it wasn't even six o'clock yet. I hadn't made any money yet to go to the prison store to buy anything to read or anything to write with so I just laid down in my bed. I couldn't sleep so I had nothing to do but sit there and gather my thoughts together about my first day.

I had survived but with a new enemy I felt that my days were numbered. How could I possibly avoid this woman and her gang? I thought back to the original threat and couldn't think of any way that I had brought this on. I hadn't even made eye contact with her. She was just looking for a fight and felt that she could handle winning one with me.

I remembered back to the last time I was threatened and force to fight someone. It was back in middle school. I was only

29

thirteen at that time. I remembered the girl as she came up to me in the hallways in between classes. She was intimidating but I didn't fear anyone back then. I've always been a survivor and could handle myself well.

Apparently, this girl from school had been after me for weeks. She had a crush on a boy that ended up having a crush on me and this didn't sit well with her. I didn't even notice that the boy existed. But she shoved me. The next thing I knew I was over top of her pounding away and there was a circle of kids surrounding us cheering me on. I figured I'd keep swinging and hitting until someone stopped me. Eventually, someone did.

A teacher came from behind me and pulled me off of her. I was still swinging for a few moments as I was being pulled up. I was taken down to the principal's office from there and they attempted to call my Aunt but never did get a hold of her. My younger sister and I were raised by my Aunt from the time I was six years old and she was only two.

By the time school ended, they still hadn't had any success at contacting my Aunt so one of the teachers volunteered to take me home. As we pulled up in front of my Aunt's trailer, a few of her kids were running around the yard and squirting each other with water guns. They were half naked and filthy as always and the teacher looked disgusted by the site. There was trash piled up at the end of the trailer and my Aunt came walking out of the front door holding one of her babies and yelling at the kids to quiet down.

My Aunt was always drinking and never paid much attention to the children unless she was yelling at them. My teacher got out of the car with me and walked up to the front of the trailer to explain to my Aunt why she was bringing me home. As we approached, my Aunt turned around and looked the teacher up and down before saying, "What's she done this time? The little monster's always causing some kind of trouble."

The teacher tried to politely explain, "Roxanne was caught fighting in school. It's not really a big deal. Kids will be kids. But, she has been suspended for three days as a result so I'll need you to attend a parent/teacher conference in order to get her back in school by this Thursday. It's scheduled for Wednesday afternoon. Can you attend?"

My Aunt didn't look very pleased by this news but responded, "Well, at least I'll have a babysitter for the next three days. I need a break from these kids. And as far as the meeting goes, I'll be there. What choice do I have?" She went back inside the trailer and slammed the door behind her. My teacher looked at me and said, "Well, I drove you home. That's all I was expected to do. See you in school on Thursday." At that, she walked back to her car as fast as she could and left me standing there on the front porch to the trailer.

That was the only fight I had actually been in before and I handled myself fairly well with it. I decided that I had nothing to fear by the bully I was facing in prison. I would just have to apply the same principles as I did before. Just start swinging like a mad woman. I was bound to get a hit in somewhere.

Over the next hour, the prisoners continued to file into their cells, doors slamming one after another and eventually everything quieted down. It must have been after seven o'clock by the time the last of the prisoners were settled in and we were all in our places once again. My first day had been quite an experience but I had survived it. I fell asleep before they even called lights out.

# Chapter 4
# Crazy Chris

The whistle blew and I woke up, scrambled out of my bed and immediately began getting dressed. This was my second day and I was hoping it would go a little smoother than my first. I knew where I was supposed to be every minute of the day and had a better idea of what was expected of me. All I had to do was continue to be as invisible as possible.

I was finished with my morning chores of straightening my cell and getting dressed before most of the other prisoners I could see. I stood there facing the bars patiently as I watched the other prisoners finish up and face outward from their cells one by one. The prison guards waited until everyone was finished before they blew the whistle again and began to do the morning count.

As far as I could tell, there were several counts that occurred during the day. One count occurred as soon as we woke up and another once we arrived at our jobs. A third count occurred at the showers when they scanned each prisoner's microchip and the last count in the evening once everyone was in their cells. The Warden of this prison ran a tight ship and made it impossible for any prisoner to even think about escaping or not being where they were supposed to be at any given moment in the day.

Not only did they watch us carefully every minute of the day but the entire prison was located on an island. We were surrounded by freezing, cold water with strong currents on every side. I couldn't even imagine what would happen to a person that would even attempt to swim to the mainland, let alone what would happen if they did get caught.

Before long, we were off to breakfast and starting our day once again. It was only my second day and already I began to feel the monotony of the daily schedule. At breakfast, I met up with Jaye and we scarfed down our meal of cold cereal and milk, a small bowl of fruit and a dry piece of toast. After breakfast, we lined up to go to the courtyard and found our favorite place on the bleachers near the fence.

As we sat there together, I decided to ask more questions, "You've been here for ten years, right?" Jaye nodded and I continued, "How is it that you've managed to not make any other friends until you met me yesterday?" Jaye looked down as she replied, "I already told you yesterday why I don't talk to the other inmates. I don't want to stir up any trouble. But, I did have a best friend until about six months ago."

I knew that every prisoner in this place was serving a life sentence without the possibility for parole so I was curious about this. I asked, "What happened to her?" Jaye continued, "She had been an inmate here for years. In fact, she was one of the first of the group of inmates that was transported here from another prison back in 2050 when they opened Clausdrum. She was about my age and she never tried to start any trouble with anyone. Everyone left her alone for the most part mainly out of respect. We called her wise old Mary."

I was intrigued by this story and remained quiet as I let Jaye continue to tell me about her old friend. "One of the girls from the drug group over there was rather new here. I think she had six months in at the time. She had started to give Mary some trouble. No reason for it, really. Mary tried her best to ignore the girl and move on but it wasn't enough. Mary was walking back to her cell from the showers one night when this girl came up from behind and shoved her. Mary wasn't one to take something like that and not fight back, so she turned around and hit the girl. During the fight, the girl grabbed Mary by the hair and started banging her head against the wall. Mary couldn't break free from her grip but the guard came down and stopped the fight soon after it started and sent them both to solitary confinement."

Jaye paused for a moment and looked as if she might tear up while telling me this story and I started to regret asking. I still wanted to know what had happened to her. "So, what happened after that?" Jaye replied, "Well, she went to solitary but no one thought to have the Nurse check her out before throwing her in that place. By the next morning, when they did their rounds, she was dead. Apparently, she had some damage done from when the girl banged her head against the wall. She went to sleep and never woke up."

I was shocked by the story that Jaye had told me and I was curious to know if this happened often. Jaye continued to explain that new procedures were put in place from that incident and each time inmates get into a physical fight, they are checked out by the Nurse before being sent to solitary. I attempted to sound encouraging, "I guess some good came of it." Jaye didn't seem very pleased by my statement. She said, "Yeah, it's a real blessing in disguise."

I was quiet for a few minutes before I finally said, "I'm sorry to hear about your friend." Jaye shrugged and said, "It's okay. People die in this place. Maybe she's happier now." As we continued to sit there observing the other groups of women from a distance, I couldn't help but stare at Crazy Chris and study her movements. She was in her corner just like she was yesterday, just mumbling to herself and rocking back and forth. I felt sorry for her. She seemed to be lost in her own world, completely oblivious to her surroundings.

I decided to try something new. I stood up and walked over toward where she was sitting. I was going to try and talk to her. Jaye yelled to me as I began walking over there but she obviously didn't want to draw any attention to herself. She hurried over to walk along side me. As I continued in that direction, Jaye said, "Roxy, what are you doing? You can't just go over and talk to her. She's been here for as long as I have and stuck in this state of insanity for too long."

I ignored her and kept on walking toward Crazy Chris. I stopped right in front of her and sat down. She froze. She stopped mumbling and sat extremely still and stared straight ahead. After a couple of minutes I said, "My name is Roxy. What's yours?" Nothing. She continued to stare straight ahead. Jaye just stood there next to me with nervousness as she looked around the courtyard and obviously wondered what other people thought about this. I could see a few of the other inmates staring at me as if I were making a scene but I wanted to know what was wrong with this girl.

I asked again, "What's your name?" Jaye finally said to me, "Roxy, come on. Let's go back over and sit down. She's not going to talk to you." I sighed as I realized Jaye was right. This girl really was insane. There was no hope for someone like this. Maybe she was crazy before she killed her parents. That's probably why she did it in the first place.

I reluctantly gave up and walked back over to the bleachers with Jaye. As we walked toward our area, Jaye yelled out to the other inmates, "What are you all staring at? There's nothing to see here!" The guards in the tower were now looking down at the scene as well. Jaye quietly mumbled to me, "You're going to get us in so much trouble. What did I tell you about making waves?" We just sat there quietly for the rest of our time in the courtyard before it was time for lunch.

35

After lunch, I reported to the Cell Block area for my job just as I had the day before. The other four girls were there already by the time I arrived but I still made it on time with two minutes to spare. Once we were down in the lower level, we grabbed our bins, took them to the clothing room and began folding.

As I was folding the clothes in my bin, the drug girl came over to me once again and said, "You trying to bully someone that can't fight back?" At first I didn't know what she was talking about. When she saw the blank look on my face she explained, "You were trying to bully Crazy Chris, weren't you? I knew you were trouble from the moment I laid eyes on you. Your ass is mine. You won't know when and you won't know where but I'm watching you."

The guard at the doorway yelled to keep us from talking. She went back over to her bin and continued folding as she glared at me the entire time. I couldn't believe what I was hearing. At that point, I knew that she was just looking for an excuse to fight with me. I was definitely going to end up in solitary confinement. I just didn't know if I was going to win the fight or lose the fight. Jaye couldn't possibly protect me all the time so I had to be ready for it.

After I took my shower, I headed to my cell and spent the rest of the night thinking about the events of the day and dreading the next. I fell asleep rather quickly and woke to the sound of the whistle blowing the very next morning at six o'clock sharp. I went through the same routine of getting dressed, cleaning my cell and heading to breakfast. After breakfast, we all lined up for the courtyard.

As I sat down on the bleachers with Jaye, we started talking right away as usual and I assumed today was going to be just like any other. But as we sat there talking, Crazy Chris walked straight past her usual spot and toward us instead. We were stunned as she kept walking toward us.

She came right over and sat down on the bleachers next to me. Jaye was sitting to my right and Crazy Chris sat down to my left. She wasn't much better of course. She continued to mumble quietly to herself and rock back and forth but she was sitting with us.

Jaye and I just sat there for the longest time and stared at the sight. We didn't know what to say. Then, we both started laughing. We couldn't believe it. Jaye said, "After ten years of sitting in that same spot, she finally decided to sit somewhere else." I smiled and added, "She's sitting with us."

I looked over toward her and said, "I'm glad to see your venturing from your routine a bit. Are you going to tell me your name now?" She continued to mumble to herself and didn't acknowledge my question at all. But I really was glad to see that she had made a little progress and changed her routine. I didn't care that she mumbled to herself. I just didn't want her to be alone anymore and she wasn't. She had us to keep her company from that day forward.

As we sat there for a little while longer, we noticed that the drug girls were glaring over at us. Jaye noticed it right away and said, "What do you think that's all about?" I replied, "The one that I do laundry duty with threatened me yesterday and accused me of bullying Crazy Chris." Jaye looked shocked. "So, you gave them a reason to fight?" I didn't respond to that. I felt that I hadn't done anything wrong. Surviving in this place was a lot like walking on egg shells. One wrong move and someone is after you, not to mention trying to keep the guards off your back.

As we sat there and avoided eye contact with the drug girls, a few of them started walking over toward us. As they came closer, I could see the one I worked with every day. They looked as if they were definitely going to cause trouble. As they approach us and stood in front of me, the one that had been threatening me did all the talking. She looked right at me and said, "What did I tell you about bullying people who can't fight back?" I had no idea what she was talking about so I didn't respond.

37

"Maybe you didn't hear me the first time. I said, why are you bullying this girl and making her sit with you? She doesn't want to sit here." How could she possibly know that? Crazy Chris was the one who came over to us. All I did was open that door and welcome her. I realized right away that this was just an excuse to start something and I did not want to go to solitary. As I continued to ignore her comments, it seemed that her energy level continued to rise as she began using hand gestures as she spoke, "You want to fight someone? Come on then and fight me! I can fight back and win with your skinny ass!"

I couldn't take anymore. One thing I had never learned in my life was to control my anger. I had a short fuse and I was ready to snap at that moment. I stood up and found myself two inches from her as I said in the calmest voice I could, "I don't want to fight anyone, not even you. I want no trouble and as far as Chris is concerned, she came over and sat with us. No one is making her sit here." I wanted to say more but as I was speaking, I heard the whistle blow and guards yelling as they ran over toward us.

I never thought I'd be glad to hear that whistle but it was my saving grace at that moment. As soon as the guards came running, I backed off and sat back down on the bleachers. Even though I was obviously not a threat at this moment, the guards stood between the two of us and one of them said, "Do I need to put the two of you in solitary? You know the rules. Play nice!"

One of the guards herded the drug girls back to their normal place and I remained seated on the bleachers as the other guard stared me down. He looked at the number on my yellow jumpsuit as he said, "Are we going to have a problem with you, number CL15595?" I shook my head but never made eye contact with him.

He walked away and I sat there in disbelief at how unfair the rules were in this place. I was the one that was attacked and the guards gave me no protection. In fact, they acted as if I were just as guilty as drug girl. Jaye remained quiet for the rest of our time in the courtyard and Crazy Chris just sat there staring straight ahead.

After lunch, we went our separate ways to go to our jobs. I arrived at my normal place with a few minutes to spare and met up with Officer Yander. I was the second person to arrive and drug girl wasn't there yet. I was dreading her arrival as I stood there waiting to start my work. One of the other women came around the corner and upon seeing her, Officer Yander said, "Okay, that's everyone. Let's get going."

I was surprised. Drug girl hadn't arrived yet and there were only three of us. I couldn't help myself from asking, "Wait, there should be one more. Where's the other girl?" Officer Yander didn't look very pleased with the fact that I was holding up work by asking questions but answered anyway, "Oh, you mean your friend, Shelly? She's been reassigned. I know it breaks your heart but you won't be working together anymore. Can't keep the two of you separated." I could hear the sarcasm in his voice but I was ecstatic at what he had just said.

Now I knew I had nothing to worry about since I wouldn't be near her anymore. I felt safe for the first time since I had arrived. Obviously, the guards were looking out for me. Plus, they did respond very quickly in the courtyard, which surprised me. The only guard I had seen prior to the whistle blowing was the guard at the entrance to the building. I had no idea where the other guards had come from and didn't give much thought to it. I decided not to ask any more questions about it. I simply followed the others down the stairs to the clothing room.

After our work day was completed and we were told to stop folding clothes, Officer Yander instructed us all to raise our left arms. He took a scanner out and scanned each one of our microchips. I was confused as to why we were being scanned so I asked, "What's this about?" Officer Yander continued scanning the others as he answered my question, "Its Friday and Friday is payday. You're being awarded for your hard work with credits you can use in the prison store."

This was the first time I had given the prison store much thought. I didn't even know where it was located or when we would even have the chance to go buy things when we were on such a strict schedule. I then asked, "When can we go buy things?" For the first time, Officer Yander acted as if he were human and not some programmed machine that didn't make eye contact.

He looked at me and chuckled as he answered, "You go during your 'free time' in the courtyard. All you have to do is walk up to the guard at the entrance to the building and request to go to the prison store. Another prison guard will escort you there and back."

Then, I wondered how many credits I had received but refrained from asking. I didn't want to push my luck with getting answers from the guard. We filed out of the clothing room and back upstairs for dinner. I thought about what I would like to purchase in the prison store and what types of things they had available. I had seen other inmates reading and writing in their cells.

I figured they'd probably have paper, envelopes and stamps for writing letters to people on the outside. Even though it's unheard of nowadays for people to actually write letters to each other, it was still the only means of communication with anyone on the outside. They also allowed visitors so you could see family in person during visiting hours.

I knew that no one would ever come to visit me but I thought about writing a letter to my Aunt. I hated her and everything about her. I knew that she wouldn't care if I wrote a letter to her. The more I thought about it, the more I figured she would probably throw my letter away without even opening it.

I was absolutely certain that she felt the same way toward me as I felt toward her. However, I had no one else to contact. I felt sad about that but it was the way things were and I certainly couldn't do anything to change it. I had to make a conscious effort to not dwell on my problems or feel sorry for myself.

After dinner, we all went to take our showers and, as I was coming out of the changing room to get my shoes, the drug girl, Shelly, was walking by to take her shower next. As she passed by me, she said, "You think you can get rid of me that easy? When I get a hold of you, there won't be anything left! Thanks to you, I'm now on trash duty!" I shuttered at the thought of what trash duty entailed and shuttered more at the thought of fighting Shelly now that she was really mad. I ignored the comment and headed back to my cell for the night.

As I sat in my cell, I saw Jaye going into her cell just moments after I had arrived in mine. I went to the bars of my cell and yelled over to her to get her attention. She looked up and I said, "Shelly's on trash duty now." Jaye seemed happy by this news as she responded, "Well, that's one place she won't be able to get you." I smiled and sat back down on my bed. I still had nothing to read or do so I just sat there with only my thoughts and the noise of the other inmates to occupy my time. Although Shelly had been moved to another job, her threat at the showers continued to haunt me.

That night I hardly slept as I thought about Shelly coming after me. Even when I did manage to finally get to sleep, I would have a nightmare about it and wake back up again. After spending the entire night tossing and turning and worrying about my future, I finally got up at about five thirty and started quietly cleaning my cell. After the first whistle of the day blew, I was ready and facing outward at my cell bars five minutes before anyone else.

For the next couple of days, I continued to look over my shoulder for Shelly at all times. At each meal, in the courtyard and after showers, I watched for her. I knew that the places she could attack me were very limited but, if there was a way, she would definitely find it.

She glared at me anytime she saw me and if she had the chance she would threaten me. She wanted to scare me and it was beginning to work. I was losing sleep over this every night as I tossed and turned and wondered when and where I would be attacked.

# Chapter 5
# The Escape

Over the course of the next week, Crazy Chris continued to sit next to me during our time in the courtyard. Jaye and I would talk and Crazy Chris would just sit there and mumble quietly to herself. Eventually, she stopped mumbling as much and spent more time listening to Jaye tell me everything she knew about the prison. Jaye had learned quite a lot of information about this building from her old friend Mary.

According to Jaye, the building we occupied had been there for two hundred years. In fact, she told me that it was a prison for men a long time ago. From what she knew, it had been built in the eighteen hundreds and was originally used to house prisoners of war. Eventually, when the war was over, they converted it to a maximum security prison for men. It was called Alcatraz during that time.

She spoke to me about some of the history that she knew in regards to the old Alcatraz site. For instance, Jaye had heard that the original prison was famous for being impossible to escape. Apparently, many escape attempts were made but most of them failed. She also knew that Alcatraz housed some of the most dangerous criminals of that time, which included gangsters and boot bootleggers of the twentieth century and even a train robber.

I was amazed by these stories that Jaye had heard, but I wasn't absolutely convinced that any of them were true. However, listening to the stories did help to pass the time. Jaye had continued to explain that the prison was eventually shut down and turned into a museum. I couldn't understand why any prison would become a museum. Why would someone want to voluntarily visit a prison that had been shut down? I asked why the prison was shut down but Jaye said she wasn't sure the reason either.

By the year 2035, all the states in our country had completely abolished the death penalty. Texas was the last to reluctantly eliminate this as a punishment for dangerous criminals. Apparently, there were many groups that protested death as a punishment for dangerous people.

I don't think I would have protested it if I had lived during that time. Even though I was a criminal, I'm sure the people protesting had never had a loved one taken from them at the hands of someone dangerous. However, all of the criminals that were on death row at that time automatically received a life sentence without the possibility of parole.

On top of that, there had been a steady rise in violent crimes among women, which created a problem with more women receiving a life sentence. The nature of the crimes that women were beginning to commit more and more resulted in the increased need for maximum security prisons for women. The prisons they had were becoming overcrowded very quickly.

Furthermore, the invention of the Mini Sirens in the year 2040 prevented criminals from escaping and assisted the police in tracking down suspects much quicker than they had been able to before. Jaye had even said that there used to be something called a Bounty Hunter and that their job was to travel around the world hunting people down who had warrants out on their arrest. Sometimes it took years to locate one person and criminals could outsmart the police much easier in those days.

As I listened to all the history that Jaye had told me, I couldn't even imagine living in that day and age. It must have been so hard on the average person. In fact, it even sounded a little barbaric to me with having criminals running lose in the streets and police traveling the world in search for a suspect.

Even though I had committed a crime that landed me in a maximum security prison, I couldn't imagine having criminals running free. I felt it would have been such a chaotic and dangerous world to live in one hundred years ago. I had trouble believing everything Jaye had told me but I didn't let her know that I doubted her stories.

Apparently, Alcatraz was remodeled and reopened in the year 2050. They renamed the site Clausdrum. This allowed for more room to house the women being convicted of violent crimes. Jaye's friend Mary had already been serving a life sentence in a Louisiana prison when the doors to Clausdrum were opened. Mary was one of the prisoners in the first group of three hundred women brought to the island in September of 2050.

The Warden of Clausdrum was an older man in his late sixties and was more than qualified to handle the prison well. He was originally in the Military and moved up the ranks fairly quickly while serving his time with the Marines. Eventually, he retired after spending twelve years as a Drill Sergeant and became a Warden of a prison in California.

He was extremely successful at running the prison he was in charge of and was more than qualified to run Clausdrum. When Jaye told me he was a Drill Sergeant in the Marines, I could definitely believe it by the way he was running Clausdrum. It felt like a Marine boot camp to me with the extremely rigid schedules and strict rules.

As the week went on and I listened to Jaye's stories, I also observed Crazy Chris. One day we were sitting outside and Jaye

45

was rambling on about the history of the prison when I noticed that Crazy Chris wasn't mumbling nearly as much as she had been. In fact, she had even stopped rocking back and forth.

I interrupted Jaye to focus her attention on the girl but Jaye wasn't as impressed as I was. I asked Crazy Chris, "Hey, you gonna tell me your name yet?" She only stared straight ahead. I tried again, "You gonna tell me anything about yourself?" She responded in a soft voice, "No." She then went right back to mumbling to herself. Jaye and I both shook our heads and went back to talking with each other.

As I continued to watch Crazy Chris, I wondered to myself why I even cared. I was going to spend the rest of my life in this place for good reason. I'm not supposed to have a heart for some strange girl who seemed perfectly content with her life before I showed up. But I realized that she reminded me so much of my younger sister, Kate, minus the insanity.

Kate was my life at one point. She was four years younger than me. When our mother had run out on us, I was six and Kate was only two years old at that time. Neither of us had fathers that could take us in. My father had been serving a life sentence in a penitentiary in Maryland for murder and I had never met him. He was sentenced to life right before I was born and I never had any desire to know more than that.

Kate never knew who her father was. Our mother had many boyfriends and wasn't much of a motherly type. However, I do have a few memories of moments where she had spent quiet time with me before my sister was born. I always felt bad that Kate never even got to experience that with our mother. She had a drug addiction that she just couldn't overcome and tended to put her boyfriend's ahead of us.

After my mother left us, the government had to find a place for us to live. We didn't want to be split up and the next of kin for us was an Aunt who already had six children of her own. It didn't take long for me to realize that her six kids were not well cared for. Our Aunt was an alcoholic and her six children basically had to fend for themselves. They were rarely bathed or fed. They missed school quite often and had absolutely no discipline in their lives.

I guess I took Kate under my wing, so to speak, and she became my world from that moment on. Together we survived our childhood the best way we knew how. She was very dependent on me most of the time. Even though I wasn't much older, I became sort of like a mother to her. I made our lunches for school each day, helped her with her homework and made sure we had dinner each night. There were times that I had to steal food for us and other times when we went to the neighbors and begged. I wasn't proud of any of it but we had to survive somehow.

I never became very close to any of my six cousins we were forced to live with. As far as I was concerned they were brats and they hated us. They would say things like, "You're only here because the government wouldn't take you." or "Your mother is a whore." I yelled at one of my cousins when he insulted my mother, but my Aunt threatened to send us to foster care where Kate and I would probably be split up. From that moment on, we kept our distance and ignored them. At least we had a place to sleep each night and we were together.

That was our life growing up and the only life we had ever known. I became a survivor and Kate became dependent on me to help her survive. I guess my life really hadn't changed much since then and now I had Crazy Chris to look after. My life would be exactly the same. The only difference was that, at least in prison, I was guaranteed three hot meals every day.

After I had been in the prison for approximately two weeks, Jaye and I were sitting in the courtyard talking while Crazy Chris sat beside me just listening. Jaye was continuing to tell us stories of what Clausdrum had been at one time when Crazy Chris spoke. At first I couldn't hear what she was saying but I knew right away that it wasn't senseless mumbling. Jaye must have thought so too

47

because she stopped talking, stared at Crazy Chris and said, "Did she just say something?"

"They're going to escape." Crazy Chris repeated as she continued to stare straight ahead. I asked, "Who's going to escape? Are you talking about the stories Jaye has been telling? There just stories. None of them are true." I could see Jaye giving me a bit of a glaring look as I said this. However, before any of us could react, loud sirens began going off. Everyone was on alert as the sound was deafening. By the looks of it, none of the other prisoners knew what was going on around us as their eyes darted about with confusion.

Then, Jaye yelled and pointed down toward the water's edge to the left, "Look! There are prisoners down there!" I looked toward that direction and beyond the fence there were four women in yellow jumpsuits running as fast as they could toward the ocean. Right behind them, about twenty yards or so, I could see the Mini Sirens racing toward them. The Mini Sirens were gaining speed and moving at a faster rate than the women. They were closing in on the women rather quickly.

Just before they reached the edge of land, I saw something small fly through the air toward them and land in the shoulder of one of the prisoners. She had been hit with a Tazer Dart and fell to the ground immediately as the electricity coursed through her body for about twenty seconds. This gave a couple of the guard's time to rush up and restrain her while a few other guards raced after the remaining women in a Rover Cart. Two of the women were jumped by the guards and wrestled to the ground but one of the women actually dove into the ocean before any of the guards could catch her.

We all stood there at the fences edge and watched the entertainment being carried out before us. None of the guards seemed to notice as we were all so intrigued by the attempted escape. Every guard was focused on the escapees and doing

48

everything they could to catch each one of them. We continued to watch.

The guard that had been chasing the one that got away began stomping the ground and yelling. He turned and started yelling orders to the other guards. We couldn't hear anything they were saying from this distance but two of the other guards ran toward a small boat with bright orange floatation devises on each side and a motor in the back. Jaye later explained that this type of boat was called a floater and is used frequently by Military and Police for jobs such as this.

The two guards took the small boat out into the water in search of the woman that got away while the other guards took their prisoners back toward the main entrance. As we stood there watching the rest of the show, the voice of one of the guards began yelling over the speakers from behind us, "Step away from the fence and move back to the courtyard." We reluctantly did as we were told.

After we were back on the bleachers again, I wondered how Crazy Chris knew they were going to escape. I asked Jaye what she thought and she replied, "I guess she must have seen them or something." I wasn't sure if that was true but I didn't want to argue. I changed the subject, "So, do you think that one woman will get away?" Jaye replied, "No. Even if she did manage to make it across a freezing ocean with strong currents, she has a tracking devise. We all do. It's only a matter of time before they find her and bring her back. And probably not much time."

Jaye was right. No one could ever escape prison. It was impossible because the Mini Sirens would track you before you even had the chance to enjoy any amount of freedom. On top of that, it was November and the water would be freezing. If the current didn't pull her down, the cold water would definitely slow her down and the Mini Siren's would track her in no time. I realized at that moment that none of us would ever have a chance at being free again, even if we were crazy enough to attempt an escape.

For the remainder of that day, there was heaviness in the air. At first I didn't understand why, but after a while, I realized what it was. Everyone else had come to the same conclusion I did about the possibility of escaping this place. We all knew that there was no hope of getting out alive.

I didn't see what had happened to the women that had gotten caught and wasn't sure if I'd want to know. They were on a different work schedule than me so I had never met them or seen them before. I figured they were being punished for their attempt to gain freedom. I also pondered the possibility that perhaps the fourth woman may have drowned in the ocean.

I couldn't understand how they had gotten out in the first place. There had to have been a guard watching over them just like we had in the afternoon. I couldn't figure out how they could possibly have gotten out of sight. There just was no way to shake the guards that constantly watched us. Then, I realized that the woman who jumped into the ocean may have faced a better fate than the other three that were caught. It was better to die trying than to get caught by the guards.

After my work was done and I headed to dinner, I continued to think about what I had seen earlier that day. I was given my dinner and I sat down next to Jaye. Once we began eating, Jaye said, "I got word on what happened with the attempted escape today. The Nurse and the guards were all talking about it while I was working in the hospital."

I couldn't wait to hear what she knew. "What happened?" I asked. Jaye continued, "Apparently, all four of the women were working in the receiving dock. That's where the supplies are delivered each week from the mainland. They must have been planning it but without warning all four of them took off running as fast as they could. I'm not sure why they thought they'd be able to escape. Maybe this place got to them and made them lose their minds."

I was curious on what the consequences were for attempting to escape since I hadn't seen anything about that in the pamphlet I had received when I first arrived. "What's going to happen to them now?" Jaye sighed and said, "Well, I'm not sure. The last time someone tried to escape, they ended up going into Cell Block D. It was really strange because Cell Block D is for the really violent inmates that aren't allowed to be with the rest of us. I thought they'd send the woman to solitary for a while or something but they didn't. I'm not sure if there was something else going on with that or not. Never did get the whole story."

I finished my dinner and we were herded downstairs for our showers. As I was in line and approaching the shower room I heard yelling from behind me, "Step to the side! Coming through! All prisoners against the wall!" I did as everyone else did and pressed my back up against the wall as I saw two guards coming through with a woman wrapped in a fleece blanket.

I didn't get a good look at the woman who had jumped into the ocean earlier because of the distance but I would guess that this was her. She was shivering and her lips were a little blue as they hurried her down the corridor. They rushed passed us and into the shower room where they stripped her down and put her under one of the shower heads.

We had to wait in the hallway outside the shower room for another fifteen minutes before they guided her back over toward the clothing room. We all remained rather quiet as we waited to be told to take our showers. Eventually, the guards began herding us once again and our schedule went back to normal. I didn't see the woman again that night and I didn't hear anything else about the escape.

I went to bed wondering what was going to happen to them. I just couldn't understand why they thought they could get away.

51

After giving it some thought, I came to the same conclusion as Jaye; this place could make a person lose their sanity. Maybe that's what had happened. Perhaps they just couldn't take anymore. They must have known that jumping into the cold ocean water would mean certain death. I guess after being here for so long, certain death seems welcoming.

As I fell asleep that night, I thought about the entire events of the day. I dreamed about the four women that had escaped. However, in my dream they all jumped into the water and drowned themselves. I stood there at the water's edge as I saw each of their bodies floating upward toward the surface of the water. They were free.

# Chapter 6
# New Co-Worker

The next day, I actually awoke rather refreshed after a good night's sleep. We went through our normal routines of cleaning, dressing, then breakfast. Jaye and I sat in our usual place during our free time in the courtyard and Crazy Chris sat right alongside us listening to every word we said.

"So, you never said what you did to get a ticket into this hell hole. What crime did you commit?" Jaye inquired. I wasn't afraid to talk about it, so I didn't hesitate to tell her. "I killed a man who deserved to die." I looked Jaye in the eyes and continued, "And I would do it again, given the chance." Jaye smiled and didn't ask any more questions about it.

After lunch, we went to our jobs. I had gotten there early as usual and stood with one of the other women and Officer Yander while we waited for the last woman to show up. After waiting for about another minute, two women came around the corner to meet up with us. Apparently, we had a new member in our group to replace Shelly. I recognized the new person and knew that she wasn't as much of a  threat as Shelly had been.

She was one of the lesbians that sat at the picnic tables in the courtyard during the morning hours. As soon as they were standing beside us, Officer Yander instructed her that we would be folding the clothes and led us all down to the lower level where we grabbed our carts and followed him into the clothing room. Once we were inside the room, Officer Yander continued to give instructions on what to do. I realized at that moment that Officer Yander makes it a habit to give instructions any time we have a new member. That must have been the reason he did so on my first day.

Once we were folding the clothes, the woman from the lesbian group quietly introduced herself to me. "Hi, I'm Kerry. I've seen you out in the courtyard before." I was nervous about her speaking to me. For one, I didn't want to give her mixed signals and end up being her girlfriend. On top of that, I was nervous about Officer Yander. He had yelled any time Shelly tried to speak to me before and I expected him to do the same this time. I was surprised to see that he didn't.

I'm sure he could hear her talking from where he was sitting but he just sat there reading something from his tablet. In that moment, it occurred to me that Officer Yander knew that Shelly was a problem and a threat. That was the sole reason he had yelled at Shelly for talking to me. I felt safe knowing that the guards were secretly looking out for me. At least some of the guards were focused on my safety and that was better than being completely on my own.

I smiled and said, "I've seen you too. You sit at the picnic tables." I didn't make eye contact while speaking with her. She looked at me as she responded, "Yes, I do sit at the picnic tables, but I'm not gay." I stopped folding for a moment and studied her face to try and see where she was going with this. She looked away as she continued to fold clothes from her bin.

She was an average sized woman of about forty years old. She had short hair that looked as if she had cut it herself, even though I knew she probably had gotten her hair cut at the chop shop. We did have a place somewhere in the prison where we could use our credits to get a haircut. It's not much of a beauty shop but I've heard inmates refer to as the 'chop shop'.

I went back to folding as well while I tried to absorb what she had just told me and she continued to explain, "I've been here for three years and I didn't know anyone when I got here. I was scared and wanted to fit in somewhere in order to ensure my own protection in this place. I noticed right away that no one messed with the lesbians and they were nice enough. So, I began sitting with them every day."

I couldn't believe what I was hearing. This woman had sold herself out to a group in order to ensure her own safety. At that moment, I was extremely grateful that I had met Jaye. I responded, "Well, you can sit with us if you want to, as long as it would be okay with your girlfriends."

Kerry, explained, "Oh, they're not my girlfriends, other than the fact that I sit with them every day. I have managed to play things off so to speak. I don't even know if they are aware of my existence sometimes. I would love to sit with you." I smiled and we worked quietly for the rest of the day.

After we were finished with our work, we headed back upstairs to the main level to get dinner. Once we were in the cafeteria, I lost tract of Kerry but I continued through the line as usual. I figured if she wanted to find us, she would. I was right.

As soon as I sat down next to Jaye, Kerry came walking over to our table with her tray. I was surprised when I saw that Crazy Chris was walking alongside her. She came up to the table and said, "Look who I found. She was sitting way over in the corner all by herself."

They both sat down and I felt good about the new group that was forming. We were starting our own little gang here in prison. The only difference was the fact that our gang welcomed new members and we didn't pick fights with the other groups.

55

I figured that we're all here for the rest of our lives so we'd better make the best of it. I looked at Kerry and asked, "So, what are you here for?" Kerry didn't seem to mind that I had asked this question and she answered in between taking bites of her food. "Well, a little more than three years ago, I killed my ex-boyfriend." Her answer seemed straight forward enough to me.

She continued, "We had been dating for about five years off and on. We would break up because he thought I was too clingy and controlling. But eventually, we'd get back together again. One time when we had broken up, I followed him from work expecting him to go home. He didn't. He went straight to someone else's house. I peered in through the window to see who he was with and saw that it was another woman."

Right away, I could see where this was going and realized that she had been a stalker. She continued to talk about it, "I went back to my car and grabbed my handgun. I went marching into the house and shot him dead." When she saw the surprised expressions on our faces, she stopped eating and defended herself, "What? He was with another woman."

Jaye and I quickly went back to eating and Jaye changed the subject. "So, Roxy, have you heard any more about the prisoners who tried to escape yesterday?" I hadn't and shook my head, knowing by the look on Jaye's face that she had new information on it. She wouldn't bring it up unless she knew something. "Well, I heard the Nurse and the guard talking again today while I was working. They said the prisoners are in solitary."

"So, the punishment for such a crime is solitary." I said. Jaye continued, "It is. Apparently, it's going to be longer than a week but they'll eventually be put back into the general population again." I commented, "I wonder why that one woman you told me about ended up in Cell Block D permanently?" Jaye shrugged her shoulders as to say she had no idea.

Kerry intervened at that moment, "I remember her. That was about two years ago, wasn't it? I had heard that she was originally supposed to be in Cell Block D but there was some mess up with the paperwork and she mistakenly was put with the general population."

I could tell right away that this was news for Jaye as she studied our new member for a moment after the comment. Jaye finally said, "I like you. You've gotten more gossip than I've gotten on it. Maybe you know the answers to other things. At least we could use you as a bit of a spy to get information if we ever need it." Kerry looked a bit uncomfortable with this but I just remained quiet and finished my dinner.

Later that evening, after shower time was over, I laid there in my bed as I stared up at the ceiling. I still had not gone to the prison store by this point but figured I had the rest of my life to do so. I wasn't in a hurry. I just laid there and thought about my life before prison and the people I used to know.

I wondered what would have happened if things hadn't turned out the way they did. What if I had never killed Wesley? Then, I realized that if things hadn't have gone the way they did, my little sister probably would have ended up in a prison like this one. The more I thought about it, the less doubt I had about her future if things went slightly different than they did.

Kate was always a good kid when we were growing up. She was very compliant and quiet. She never made waves in school and always did her homework. She was very smart and had a lot of potential. I thought she had a bright future and I would have done anything to make it possible for her to attend college after high school. I was always proud of her when she was young. However, things changed when she turned thirteen.

When Kate started middle school, she made some new friends that I never approved of. Since we were raised in such a tough area and remained in survival mode throughout our childhood, Kate had met kids who were more like us. They would steal from the local stores and get into fights at school. They were trouble from the beginning.

I remembered the arguments I would have with Kate. "Those kids are no good, Kate. You need to stay away from them." I would say. However, Kate would always respond where it hurt the most. She would say, "You're not my mother! You can't tell me what to do and who to hang out with." I knew I wasn't her mother but I did love her. I knew that she loved me as well but she was going through such a rough time.

Even so, she was right. I wasn't her mother and I had no right to tell her what to do. She changed more and more over the years. She eventually started to hang out with gang members and stay out all night long. She was coming home with large amounts of money and I knew she was selling drugs.

I continued to try and talk with her about changing her life. I was afraid that she would get caught and end up in a place like this. Worst of all, she was hanging with kids who wouldn't think twice about killing someone. Every night, I laid in bed wondering where she was and whether or not she would return home. I was afraid for her life. Then, I would begin to wonder if she could possibly take the life of another. That scared me just as much.

One time, when Kate was about seventeen years old, she had come home early. It was about midnight when I heard her come through the front door. She was crying quietly as she came in. I went out to see if everything was okay and there she was standing in the kitchen wiping her tears away.

I walked up to her and put my arm around her for comfort. She cried for a little while on my shoulder before I asked what was wrong. She backed away to tell me and that's when I saw the bruises on her face. I was mortified and angry. I asked, "Kate, who did this to you?"

At first she wouldn't tell me but eventually she said, "Wesley hit me. Remember when I told you that he was cheating on me with that slut from school?" I nodded and she continued, "Well, I confronted him about it. I just wanted to know if the rumors were true." "Did he admit to it?" I asked. She started crying again as she replied, "He wouldn't say. He started yelling at me and then he hit me."

I was furious and the next day I met up with him at his school. He was eighteen years old at the time and was a senior in high school. Kate had no idea that I was planning on confronting him and probably wouldn't have approved.

"Wesley! I have something to talk to you about." I said as I approached him. He was with a few other friends as they were leaving school and heading toward his car. "Oh, look at who it is." He said in a mocking voice. "It's Kate's big sister. Ooh, I'm scared. What are you going to do? Beat me up?" He said as his friends laughed.

I walked up to him, looked him in the eyes and said, "Are you going to give me a reason?" He laughed even harder, which made me feel small compared to him and his friends. I tried to hide my own fear as I continued, "Because if you dare to touch my sister again, I'll kill you."

At that, I walked away as they continued to laugh and make rude remarks in my direction. I really didn't think I would kill him at that time but I wanted him to be scared. Apparently, it hadn't worked. Kate came home a few more times over the next year with bruises. I guess she had gotten used to it in a way because she never cried as much as she did that first night.

She never said whether she knew I had threatened him or not but she never spoke to me again about Wesley from that day on. I had my suspicions that he had told her about the conversation we had. From that day forward, she didn't say anything to me about the beatings even when I asked. She would say, "Its none of your business. Stay out of my life." It hurt when she said these things and all I could do was hope that she would eventually move on from this jerk she called her boyfriend.

I tried to move on with my life from that point. I had gotten a job at the nearby convenient store and made just enough credits to rent a studio apartment. I didn't have much and not a whole lot of food after my rent was paid, but I would take food from the convenient store when the owner wasn't around. I never took much and I worked hard enough for it, so I didn't really consider it stealing. I was just taking the difference between what I was getting paid and what I thought I should be getting paid.

Another year had gone by and Kate was still dating this jerk when my Aunt called me. "Hello?" I said as I picked up the phone. "Roxy? It's Aunt Sis. Your sister's dead." I heard the click on the other end before I could even respond. I was in disbelief.

I was living just around the corner from where we grew up. My sister was still living with our Aunt since she was just finishing her last year of school. It was within walking distance to where I was. I headed out the door and toward my Aunt's trailer.

When I arrived, there were about three police cars and an ambulance in front of their home. Three of my cousins who were still living at home during this time were standing in the front yard with my Aunt. As I walked up to the front of the trailer to find out what was going on, they were pulling a gurney out of the home and toward the ambulance. There was a body strapped to the gurney. As I looked at the body bag that was sealed closed around what was once a person, I couldn't believe it was my sister.

I lost control at that moment. I felt like I was beside myself as my panic level reached its peak. I screamed, "Who is that? Where's my sister?" Three police officers came over to me immediately to hold me back as I ran toward the body on the gurney. I needed to know who was in the body bag.

One of the officers realized what I wanted and had compassion. He instructed the paramedics to stop and allow me to see the body. He walked me over to the gurney and one of the paramedics reluctantly unzipped the bag to show the face of the victim. It was her. It was Kate.

She laid there on the gurney staring up at nothing. Her eyes were glossed over and there was dried blood everywhere. I couldn't believe she was gone. I fell to the ground and continued to scream as loudly as I could. I glanced over at my Aunt and her children as they stood in front of the trailer staring back at me. They stood there emotionless as they watched me make a spectacle of myself.

I screamed at them, "Where were you when this happened? Why didn't you stop it? You were responsible for her!" The officer that had let me see the body replied, "No one was home when this happened. I'm so sorry for your loss but we will do everything we can to find the person that did this to your sister."

He was right about no one being home at the time. Later, I had found out that my Aunt was at her job and the other kids were out with their friends. They were older by this time and were hardly ever home. They were always out with their friends at the mall or at a party somewhere. Once I learned of this information, I did feel bad about how I reacted toward them.

However, my Aunt never seemed to care that my sister was gone. I tried to talk to her at the funeral about it and she seemed distant. She hated me from the very first day that we came to live with her and I knew it. I hated her as well. After the funeral I had less respect for her than before this had happened. I never spoke to her again from that moment on.

# Chapter 7
# Stolen Identity

The morning came rather quickly as I scrambled out of bed to the sound of the whistle blowing. After the first morning count, we headed to breakfast once again. I was glad to see that Crazy Chris came right over to our table to sit down along with our new member, Kerry. Jaye and I met up on the way over to the table.

Kerry was the first one to speak up. "So, Chris, what job do they have you assigned to?" Crazy Chris didn't respond at first and we went back to eating thinking it was a lost cause. But, after a few minutes, she said, "Dishes." I was surprised she had spoken and found myself wanting to know more about this mysterious woman. I asked, "You do the dishes after meals?" She looked straight ahead and said, "Yes, every day."

I was pleasantly surprised at the fact that Crazy Chris was now talking more. I realized right away that it must have had something to do with Kerry. Chris seemed to be much more comfortable around Kerry and was beginning to open up more and more, especially when Kerry would ask the initial question to get her talking.

After breakfast, we all filed out to the courtyard and found our spot on the bleachers. It was four of us now but we managed to stay close together after Jaye had reiterated her theory on the Recorder Spies. I wasn't about to take the chance that she was wrong. We quietly spoke more about the women who had tried to escape and wondered what they were thinking when they made a run for it.

As we were speaking more about it, Chris spoke up, "They were going to steal a floater." At first I had no idea what she meant and I asked, "What do mean by stealing a floater?" Jaye interceded, "Floaters are those small boats that I showed you the day they escaped. They're perfect for something like that because they travel so fast. They're very light weight but the engine is extremely powerful. That's why the Military and the Police use them for chases or rescues."

I remembered her pointing them out to me on the day we watched the excitement play out in front of us. She had pointed the floaters out as the guards had been boarding them and putting them into the water to go on a search for the woman who had jumped into the ocean. I suppose the women were originally going to steal the floaters to try and get to the mainland.

Kerry obviously wanted more information as well. She looked at Chris and asked, "Do you mean the women who escaped were planning on taking one of the floaters to get to the mainland?" Apparently, I wasn't the only one who had assumed this was what Chris had meant. We were all starting to understand the original plan these women had formulated. Chris replied, "Yes. The four women wanted a floater."

Kerry looked back at Jaye and me as if she had just discovered something huge. She said, "That makes so much sense. Chris used to sit at the table all the way over in the corner, before I went and asked her to sit with us. I remember seeing those women every day during mealtime. They sat at the table right beside Chris. As quiet as she is, I'm sure she heard every word they had said."

Chris probably had a lot more information on the inmates.

63

She may have had information on a lot of inmates without anyone ever knowing it. We began asking her more questions about what she knew. "The women said they would steal a floater and get to the mainland." Chris said. Kerry asked, "But they have microchips. We all do. What were they expecting to do once they got to the other side? They must have known the Mini Sirens would have tract them."

Chris continued, "They were planning to steal microchips from other people on the mainland. They wanted to switch microchips and steal identities." We were all in shock at this statement. "I can't believe they were planning to take other people's identities. It's brilliant!" Kerry had said in response to what Chris had revealed. Jaye didn't seem as impressed, "They wouldn't have had much time. The Mini Sirens are fast. The Mini Sirens would have definitely gotten to them before they got to someone else."

As they continued to debate, I asked, "Do you think they were going to kill an innocent family on the mainland or just take their microchips and let them live?" Jaye answered, "I don't think they could have let them live. I mean, just taking the microchips wouldn't have killed them and the victims would have been able to identify the four women to the police. It wouldn't be hard to catch them once they knew the true identities to trace. The police would simply plug in the information of the victims and the Mini Sirens would tract them and bring them back before night fall."

Jaye made a good point. It was decided that the women were planning on killing four innocent people in order to gain their own freedom. However, they obviously hadn't planned things out thoroughly. The police would have found the four bodies with missing microchips, then applied the same principles and would have hunted them down. It may have bought them a little bit of time, but unless they were planning on killing four more people the next day and then four more after that, the police would continue to have traced them and eventually caught up with them.

It made me cringe at the thought that they would actually

plan something so horrible, unless of course they just hadn't thought that far ahead. Either way, it was a horrific plan to begin with. Even though I was convicted for murder myself, I had a much better motive than that. At least I had a better reason to commit my crime and it wasn't a selfish one. My crime was completely out of revenge for someone I cared about and nothing more.

I remembered the day that my sister was killed and I remembered the days to follow that when I was pleading with the police for help. I went to the police the day after my sister was killed to find out if they had any information on who may have done this. After talking to the police officer at the front desk, I was taken back to the cubicles where police were working on crimes and evidence.

I was introduced to the Homicide Detective that was in charge of my sister's case. Her name was Detective Snyder. She sat me down in a chair across from her and at first I thought she really cared. She explained, "We're doing everything we can and asking questions. We're looking for clues on who may have done this to your sister. We haven't gotten any new information just yet but as soon as we do, you'll be the first to know about it."

I already knew information that they obviously didn't have. Otherwise, they would have already arrested the person responsible. I was absolutely certain of who did this crime. I said, "Have you questioned her boyfriend?" Detective Snyder looked a little surprised at my question as she replied, "I wasn't aware that your sister had a boyfriend." Great detective work, I thought to myself. I replied, "His name is Wesley Strand. They had been seeing each other for a couple of years and he used to beat her."

"I don't remember seeing anything in the police reports about her being hit by anyone." She said as she began clicking through the file on the computer in front of her. I explained, "You wouldn't. I mean, she never reported any of it. She wouldn't even talk to me about. He was cheating on her and she came home..."

Officer Snyder interrupted me, "Ms. Beatry, I know you're concerned but if the beatings weren't documented with the police department, we have nothing to go on."

I couldn't believe what I was hearing. I knew it had to be Wesley and they weren't even considering him as a suspect. He was the only one that could have killed my sister and I was sure of it. Detective Snyder must have seen the dismayed looked on my face because she continued, "Look, I'll take down that name you have and bring him in for questioning. I can't make him a suspect unless I have a reason but depending on how the questioning goes, we may just have a reason to hold him. I'll send someone to bring him in now."

She typed his name into the file, called an officer over and gave him instructions to bring Wesley in for questioning. I felt relief as I knew they were on the right tract and Wesley would end up behind bars for this. I left the precinct and waited to hear back about the case. After a couple of weeks, I hadn't heard anything. No calls, no visits from the police, nothing. Something was wrong and I knew it. I decided I'd go back to the police department and inquire about the case and find out how the questioning went with Wesley.

Once I arrived at the station, I asked specifically for Detective Snyder. I was escorted back to the same area I had been in just a couple of weeks prior when I had originally told them about Wesley. Detective Snyder came over and I asked, "Did you question Wesley?" She looked as if she had something to tell me that I wasn't going to like. "Yes, we did. He's innocent."

I was dumbfounded. "What do you mean he's innocent? Doesn't he need a jury to decide that?" Detective Snyder continued, "No, I mean, we've got no reason to even think he's a suspect in this. Ms. Beatry, he has an alibi. He wasn't at your Aunt's trailer when the murder occurred. We checked it out. It's a solid alibi."

I couldn't believe that he had an alibi. He was guilty and I knew it. I was convinced that he had someone lie for him on his whereabouts that night. I couldn't even imagine who would possibly do such a thing for him. Then I realized it must have been one of his friends that had lied in order to protect him.

He was going to walk free and enjoy his life while my sister's life was taken at such a young age. She didn't even get to graduate high school and now she was gone. I was enraged and knew I had to do something about this. I stormed out of the precinct to find him myself. I knew where Wesley and his friends would hang out and I was going to find out which one of them had lied for him, even if I had to beat it out of them.

As I approached the corner of Mayo Street, which has night clubs lined all the way to the other side and Raves that go on all night long, I saw his three friends standing at their usual hang out spot. I didn't hesitate to walk right up and start asking questions. My anger at that moment was far greater than any fear I probably should have felt.

"Where is he?" I said to one of them. They all turned toward me as one of them said, "Hey, isn't this the little girl who threatened Wesley at school? Where's who?" He said in a mocking voice. "You know exactly who!" His smile faded slightly as he leaned in and said, "You mean Wesley? He skipped town with his girlfriend yesterday. Oh, you didn't hear? He has a new girlfriend. They've actually been dating for quite a while off and on but your sister kept getting in the way."

I could hear the sarcasm in his voice and wanted to hit him as hard as I could but quickly realized how much bigger he was than me. I also realized it was pointless anyway. I wasn't after this guy. I had to remain focused on Wesley.

I chose to walk away and save my anger for Wesley. I knew they weren't going to tell me where he went so I headed for his parent's house instead. Wesley lived in a much nicer part of town and had come from a wealthy family. He had also graduated high school a year before Kate would have.

His parents probably had the means to send him to college and he'd be given the chance at a decent job and move up the company quickly. As I walked toward the neighborhood he grew up in, I began imagining how successful he would be one day. I knew I had to stop that from happening. He took my sister's future and I was determined to take his.

As I approached the front door of his parent's home, I began to feel a little nervous about what I would say. At first, I thought that I could try and convince them that I was an old friend who was looking to reconnect after quite a long time of not seeing him, but I was afraid they would notice the age difference and become suspicious. Before I really had a plan, the door swung open.

I was pleasantly surprised when I saw a small child at the door to greet me. He was about five years old and had his pajamas on. I smiled and asked, "Excuse me, but do you know where I can find Wesley?" He looked at me and replied, "You mean my brother?" I nodded and he continued, "I think he said he was going to a place called Peoria." Just then, I heard a man calling out to the boy as he was turning the corner to see who was at the door, "Joshua, what did I tell you about answering the door." He came up to the door and looked at me, "Can I help you?"

"No, thank you. I think I must have gotten the wrong house. I was looking for someone else. Sorry to bother you." I continued to apologize as I hurried down the fancy front porch and back out into the night. That was a close one. I couldn't let anyone know that I was looking for Wesley. People might get suspicious about my motives.

I hurried home and logged into my tablet to find a place called Peoria. It didn't take long. It was a small town in Illinois. It had a population of approximately two thousand people so I figured it would be rather easy to find him in such a small place.

The only problem I had at this point was how to get there. I was two states over and had no car. Everything I ever needed was within walking distance. Plus, I didn't make a whole lot so I never had the opportunity or need for a car.

I had enough to pay my rent and buy some food but not nearly enough to buy a ticket to Peoria. Once I was back at my apartment, I halfheartedly logged into my bank account anyway just hoping that maybe I had miscalculated my funds. I didn't. According to my bank account, I had twenty credits to my name. I wasn't expecting to get paid until the following Friday. I couldn't wait that long.

I decided that I needed to have a better plan. There had to be a way to make sure that Wesley did not get to enjoy his future since he took my sisters life. I fell asleep that night trying to come up with a plan on how to get there. I knew he was only two states over and it was driving me insane knowing that I couldn't get to him.

By the time morning came, I was clear minded and gave my dilemma a little more thought. Before I was done eating breakfast, I had a plan. I knew that there would be some people that would get hurt in the process, but I also realized that there was no way around that. I decided that I would start my day in the search for Wesley. All I had to do was carry out the plan without getting caught. My first step was to get the credits. After that, I would track him down. Once I found him, I'd kill him. The plan I had seemed solid enough to me.

In order to get the credits, I knew I had to steal. I had been stealing all my life so it was rather easy to come up with a plan on how to get enough credits to take on this mission. I would have to be sneaky about it so that no one would notice that it was me. First, I went to my Aunt's house. I knew that she worked during the day at the local restaurant just down the road from where she lived. As I was going to her trailer, all I could do was hope that her kids weren't at home. They should have been in school, of course, but they often times skipped.

I was relieved to see that no one was home when I arrived. I walked in, using my spare key that I still hung on to, and went straight back to her bedroom. She used to keep a shoe box with all her important information in it. I figured she would keep all her bank account information in this place as well.

I found the shoebox quickly and began rummaging through her documents. I found her bank statements with her account number written at the top. I took the first page of the statement and left as quickly as I could. Once I had the account number, I knew I needed to get to a computer and I certainly didn't want to use my own tablet just in case the police were to search my records. There was a computer library right next to the high school I used to attend and that was only about two miles from my Aunt's trailer. For me, that was walking distance and it only took me forty minutes to get there.

When I walked into the library, I looked for a computer that was hidden toward the back so that no one would see what I was doing. There were a few people there at computers but they were mostly toward the front of the library. I found a computer toward the back where no one else was sitting.

I sat down and logged into it using the number written on the edge of the computer screen. Once I was logged in, I brought up the bank's main page. I typed in my Aunt's information and quickly gained access to her account.

She really didn't have much in her account but it was a start. I began wiring the credits straight to my account. It was rather easy to wire the amount because we both used the same bank. However, I was afraid that the bank would become suspicious and call her to verify that she did wire the credits. I forced myself to not think about the worst case scenario. Besides, I was counting on the fact that she would assume she had spent all of her own credits during one of her drunken stupors. I would

70

spend the next few weeks taking a little from her at a time.

Since my Aunt didn't have nearly enough credits for me to get to Peoria, I had to continue with the second part of my plan. I would have to steal more credits from my boss. I was scheduled to work that evening and my boss was due to leave at about five o'clock, an hour after I was to arrive for my shift.

I would have the rest of the evening to give myself a little extra in my pay once he was gone. He probably wouldn't figure it out, since I wasn't planning on taking a large amount from him. Plus, my plan involved eventually leaving my job in the middle of my shift once I had enough credits to get to Peoria. I knew my boss rather well and expected that he would be more outraged at the fact that I left the store unattended than he would be at the missing credits. It was sort of a diversion, so to speak.

I left the computer library and headed home to get ready for work. I did feel a slight amount of guilt for taking my Aunt's credits but I justified it by reminding myself that she never really took care of us when we were growing up. As far as feeling bad about stealing from my boss, I told myself that he should have been paying me more than he was. I was able to ignore my own guilt by justifying my actions.

Once I was at work, I waited patiently for him to leave. I then glanced back toward his office to make sure he left the scanner behind like he normally did. He would usually leave it in his desk and lock the door before going home. He stayed right on schedule and kept to his normal routine. I saw the scanner as he placed it in the top draw of his desk just before he walked out and locked the door of his office. What he didn't know was that I had previously seen where he kept his spare key.

I waited for about an hour after he was gone to be sure that he wasn't planning on coming back for anything. Then, I carried out my plan. I grabbed the spare key from the top of the door frame and went into his office. I opened the top draw, picked up the scanner, scrolled through the employee names until I found mine. Then, I scrolled down to find the word pay, highlighted it and pressed select.

Once I had entered the amount into the scanner, I held it toward my left arm and scanned my microchip. It made a beeping sound like it normal did when it paid out but I wanted to be sure that it had worked. I logged into the computer on my bosses desk and pulled up my bank account. There it was. The amount I had just paid myself from my bosses account.

After a few weeks of stealing a little here and there, I finally had enough credits to get to Peoria and find Wesley. I left my job without telling anyone and headed straight for the bus station where I bought a ticket to Illinois. As I sat there on the bus and it began to take off, I thought I'd go find him, kill him and be back home by the day after. I never realized the adventure I had started for myself that night as I was leaving my home town.

# Chapter 8
# The New Girl

After a while of the monotonous daily schedule and the same job every day, I began to lose track of how much time I had actually been in this prison. I just knew I wasn't going anywhere anytime soon. As I laid there in my bed during the night after showers and lights out, I had trouble sleeping as I periodically thought about my life before Clausdrum.

I had been thinking about the credits I had stolen and the bus ride to Peoria to hunt down Wesley Strand as I started to drift off to sleep. Just before I was asleep for the night, I heard clanging coming from the hallways and guards yelling at someone. I opened my eyes and focused on the sound I was hearing.

At first I was scared to move, thinking maybe something was wrong but as I listened more closely, I could hear what the guards were saying. "Come on, move a little faster. Your cell is down this hall." I realized they were bringing in another prisoner. I was no longer the newest inmate of Clausdrum.

I wanted to look out through the bars to see who this person was but was afraid that the guards from the balcony would yell if they saw me out of my bed. I remembered how they had yelled at the inmates when I was being brought to my new home a couple of months earlier and I definitely didn't want to draw attention to myself in any way.

I could hear the clanging as they passed by my cell and straight down toward the end of the corridor. She was going to be in a cell to the right side of Cell Block A. I wondered what this person had done to get a ticket in this place. I was sure it probably involved murder of some sort. That seemed to be a popular theme at Clausdrum among the prisoners. After they had gotten her settled in, I laid there for a little longer wondering about the new inmate before I finally drifted off to sleep until the next morning.

The next thing I knew, I was waking up to the sound of the whistle blowing once again. As I cleaned my cell and got dressed prior to breakfast, I thought about the new girl and whether or not she knew to put her pajamas in the laundry basket and not fold them like I did on my first day. I wondered whether the guards would go easy on her if no one pointed it out. It was her first day and I didn't see any reason why they would punish someone for such a small mistake.

We lined up as usual and headed for the cafeteria. I couldn't see the new girl since my cell was closer to the cafeteria and she was behind me when we were walking in that direction. So, I made it a point to look for her once we got to the cafeteria. There were a lot of people at Clausdrum that I didn't know, but I figured I'd look for the only person who seemed to be a little lost.

Once I had my tray of food and sat down, I turned to look for the new girl. I saw her standing in the middle of the cafeteria while inmates rushed past her to find their seats. She had gotten her tray already but just stood there looking out into the crowd. After a moment, she began heading toward a table to the left side of the cafeteria. I got up from my seat, wandered over to her and said, "Hey, new girl. I wouldn't sit there if I were you." She turned toward me looking lost and confused and I couldn't help but smile knowing that I had looked just as lost only weeks before. I then said, "Come on. You can sit over here with us."

74

We walked over to our normal place where Jaye, Chris and Kerry were already sitting. I started to introduce the new person but then realized I didn't know her name. I asked, "So, what's your name?" She smiled and said, "Denise. It's nice to meet you all." She spoke with a southern accent and was polite. I knew she was going to get her ass kicked in this place.

Jaye was way ahead of me on the thought as she turned toward me and said, "We'd better keep a close eye on this one if you know what I mean." I did and I nodded in agreement. She wasn't only nice but she was also pretty.

She looked as if she had just come from a good job that required a college degree and probably had a good job prior to being put in prison. She also had good manners, which was something you never saw in prison. Since she was probably about thirty years old, I figured she had been raised with good manners and had spent the rest of her adult life perfecting them.

"So, what are in for, Denise?" Kerry asked. "I robbed a bank." Denise responded. We were all stunned as we stared at her in amazement. She smiled because she knew exactly what we were thinking. "It was an inside job." We went back to eating our breakfast but we were still in shock that she managed to rob a bank. I couldn't even begin to figure out how someone would even be able to come up with a way to do this. I knew I was going to have to get every detail of what had happened.

I had learned about old currency in history class during middle school and was always fascinated with how people used to live and survive on money. Money was something that had never existed in my lifetime. People used to carry around paper money and silver coins to exchange for items up until the twenty thirties. Prior to that, I believe they used stones.

I even remember learning that every country in the world used a different type of currency that carried different values to each. I figured a person would have to have a Master's degree just to figure out how to buy something. Depending on what country you were in and the type of money you had in your pocket, made a difference on what things cost. For example, if you had American money it would cost a certain amount but if you had European money, the same item would cost less.

Years ago, prior to my lifetime, money became obsolete. Everyone in the world began using credits. It was just after the invention of the microchip that people would have their current amount of credits held in a bank somewhere and when you purchase items the cashier would simply scan your microchip. When you did your job, your boss would pay you in credits by scanning that same microchip, which then deposited the credits immediately into your account.

I couldn't imagine living any other way. It seemed confusing just thinking about how people would have to carry around currency. Most people have their microchips just under the fatty area of the left arm. If a person is missing their left arm, they have their microchip in their right arm. If someone is unfortunate enough to not have any arms, they are forced to have the microchip implanted just under the skin on the right side of their chest.

I had also learned that back when people used money to buy things, they had to go to the banks to withdraw the money they had earned. It was much like our bank accounts now but with actual paper money. Plus, the banks in the old days used to have tellers that actually worked at each bank location. That made sense to me since someone would have to physically be there to hand over the money to the customer.

After the invention of the microchips and credits, we still had physical banks but there were no tellers. When you walked into a bank, there would be a counter with multiple screens lined up along the wall behind that counter. Each one had a teller that would communicate with the customer from a remote location. The only time someone would ever go into a bank would be to apply for a loan or question a transfer made. Otherwise, banks really never had too many customers going in and out.

The tellers actually worked at a headquarters where they would communicate with customers through the computer screens. They also did other things as well, such as manage certain accounts and update customer information that's wired directly to them via the microchip. For example, if a person gets a new job, then the HR department at that job scans their microchip in order to alert their bank so that their credits are deposited without any problems. The tellers validate all this information and constantly update accounts.

Once we were in the courtyard, we couldn't wait to ask more questions about this genius level criminal we now called our newest gang member. Jaye was quick with questions for her as she said, "So, you have to tell us. How did you manage to rob a bank?" We all leaned forward to hear her explanation.

"Well, it was quite easy, really. I worked at the bank and had come up with an idea years before I put it in place. I had a boss that was sort of a jerk and didn't really like people much. I was passed over for promotions countless times and I guess they had it coming to them." We all nodded in agreement knowing that all of our victims had it coming.

She continued, "I did have a friend who was a computer hacker. Best in the world in my opinion. He used to work for the CIA but was discharged for some stupid reason about psychiatric issues that he never really had. Anyway, he was my partner in the whole thing. I told him my idea, which was to create several small phony accounts and then have it wired to all the other accounts in the bank. Every time someone made a deposit, no matter big or small, a few credits would be transferred to our phony accounts."

We were all in amazement at this ingenious plan and hung on to every word as she continued to explain, "You see, it was such a small amount of credits that no one would even notice it was

77

gone. He said he could hack in and set it up and he did. Before we knew it, by the end of that first week, we had triple the amount we thought we would. It grew from there at such a rapid amount that we didn't know what to do with ourselves. Our plan was working perfectly."

"So, were you caught before you got to spend any of the credits?" Kerry questioned. "No, we spent a lot of the credits. It wasn't right away that my boss caught on. It had been a few months after we started our scheme. We had the accounts directly linked to our microchips. He got half the accounts and I had the other half. You know, fifty/fifty. We spent our credits on fancy dinners, shows, trips to Paris. Anyway, when I was getting paid one week, there was a glitch in the scanner and, when they scanned my arm, the scanner showed multiple accounts rather than just my own account. That's what gave us away."

"So, did you run when you knew they were on to your crime?" I asked. She continued, "No, I didn't. I've never been a criminal, really. So, I didn't think to run. Besides, for a bank robbery, they would have put the Mini Sirens on my trail in no time. The FBI gets involved with crimes like that." She was right. Stealing from the government is just about as equal to murder as far as that FBI was concerned. In fact, I wondered sometimes if stealing is considered a worse offense to them.

I never had to worry about the FBI coming after me with the small amount of credits I stole from my Aunt and my boss. I figured my boss would be more enraged at the fact that I walked out on the job, leaving the convenient store unattended than he would be about the small amount of credits I stole from his account. My Aunt would have probably thought that she had gotten drunk again and blew all her credits on alcohol. She used to get drunk regularly and not remember the night before. She would wake up and find that her account was dry and figured that she must have spent it on something.

I wasn't worried about it but even if they both had figured

out that I stole their credits, the FBI wouldn't have come after me for such a low amount. Mini Sirens cost a lot of taxpayer credits and are usually only used if a Detective or the FBI gives the command. In my case, they wouldn't have done that. It just wouldn't be worth the credits spent to chase after me for the credits I stole.

"So, have you gotten your work assignment yet?" Kerry inquired. Denise said, "Yes, I'm supposed to show up in the hallway by the visitor's station to meet up with my group for bathroom cleaning. Where do you all work?" We told her and then sympathized that she had gotten such a horrible job. "Who did you piss off?" Jaye had said. Denise didn't seem too happy about the remark but remained quiet.

Jaye spent a little time pointing out the different groups to Denise and telling her what to watch out for in the prison. She was the most knowledgeable about it and we let her take the lead in showing the new girl the ropes. She also explained the Recorder Spies and why we always sit in the same place during courtyard time. Denise seemed too smart and nice to be in a place like this one.

I couldn't help but worry about her well-being. I knew that someone was bound to try and fight her just because she doesn't seem very strong or tough. "I wonder who you're going to be working with." I said halfway to myself as I thought about how long Denise would survive. Jaye must have known what I was thinking because she added, "Hopefully, you don't have to deal with any of the drug girls. They're a tough bunch and will find a reason to fight a new person."

I couldn't understand why someone would feel the need to fight someone just because they are new. But, I figured it must have something to do with being the top dog and keeping others from picking fights with them. I glance over in that direction and saw Shelly glaring right at me.

Shelly was still on trash duty as far as I knew and she still hated me with every ounce of energy she had. I was dreading the fight but expecting it none the less. She had continued to harassed me quietly every now and then with threats. Anytime she had the chance to say anything to me, whether it was passing me in the corridor to the showers or in the cafeteria line, she would try and scare me with her words.

She obviously did not want me to forget how much she hated me. I had been watching my back the best I could and remained ready for the fight but just doing that was starting to wear on me. I couldn't spend the rest of my life watching and waiting for someone to show up and fight me. Plus, I was afraid of losing. It wasn't my ego that I was worried about. It was the outward scars that terrified me. I knew that Shelly was strong enough to do serious damage.

Shelly was a tough woman and I figured she wouldn't hesitate to use a weapon during a fight. I hadn't heard of anyone else getting into a fight with her before but the look on Jaye's face told me that I had something to worry about. I was sure that if Jaye had more information on Shelly she would have told me by now. Jaye was well aware of the threats. I kept her informed on everything that Shelly said or did to me. I guess I was secretly hoping that Jaye would fight her for me, but she never insinuated that she had any plans of doing such a thing. She just continued to have sympathy for me in the situation.

After lunch, we all went to our jobs and Kerry and I spoke a little about our thoughts on the new girl, Denise. "What do you think about her robbing a bank like that?" Kerry had asked. "It's genius. That's all I can say. It's just too bad she got caught."

My real concern was whether or not she would survive one day in this place and I voiced my opinion on this to Kerry. She agreed, "She's too nice to be here. I'm sure the drug girls are already on her tail." I added another thought, "They probably have her on the wrong job. I'm sure she's probably working with some

80

of them right now."

Officer Yander must have disapproved of what we were discussing and quieted us down, "Hey, keep folding, quietly." He said as he continued to type on his tablet. I wondered if he was actually doing work or just playing around on the tablet as we worked, but quickly decided that I didn't care either way. We went back to folding the clothes and matching up numbers.

After our work was done and we went back to the cafeteria, I became a little anxious to hear from Denise on how her job went. We all sat down and Denise came over to join us. I must not have been the only one who was eager to hear all about it because every one of us was staring at her even after the whistle blew. She began eating as if she didn't notice that we were all waiting for her to tell us, but then she finally said, "Oh, alright. I guess you all want to hear about my job." We laughed a little, as I wondered if that was allowed in prison.

She continued, "It wasn't bad at all. I work with a few inmates who could stand to use an extra bar of soap but no one bothered me that badly." We all laughed even harder. At that moment, I did notice a few of the guards moving over toward our direction as we laughed. We all simmered down and continued to eat our dinner and the guards went back to their posts.

During shower time, Shelly bumped into me once again as she said, "You'd better be ready for a fight." She was apparently planning on starting something soon, according to her threat. I was actually beginning to get a little bored with the empty threats and wished she would just get it over with. I also felt that I was letting my guard down just a bit every time I heard her tell me again how she was planning to attack me when I least expected it. Maybe they were empty threats. If she was planning on beating me up, she probably would have done it by this point.

I ignored her and went back to my cell. Once I was in my cell for the night, I laid down in my bed and began thinking about my day. I still had not gone to the prison store and wondered how many credits I had. I was afraid that I would get there and pick something out only to find I hadn't earned enough. I would be embarrassed if that were to happen, especially knowing that it would be another inmate working the scanner.

I did want to buy an envelope, paper and stamp to write a letter. That night, as I struggled to drift off to sleep, I kept thinking about writing a letter to my Aunt to apologize for stealing her credits and any other heartache I may have caused. I guess I was just desperate for someone to love me and eventually come visit. The more I thought about it, the more I realized that my Aunt would never be that person for me. Eventually, I fell asleep.

# Chapter 9
# The Hospital

Another week had gone by and nothing had changed. I was still in prison, surviving and wondering how much longer I could live this life. I had friends at this point but we were monitored so closely, it felt as if our friendship was illegal.

If we laughed too loudly, guards would glare at us in order to warn us of our behavior. Having a smile on our faces was just not acceptable. In a place like this, smiles didn't come frequently of course, but when they did, we relished in it.

I had continued to receive threats from Shelly but I had realized by this point that she was nothing but an empty threat to me. She only wanted to scare me. It worked at first but her affects were quickly wearing off. I ignored her every time she said anything to me, mainly in order to keep myself out of trouble with the guards.

Denise was getting the hang of our schedule and the rules quicker than any of us thought she would. I guess she was so polite and nice that no one wanted to pick a fight with her. I had managed to almost make it through my first day before I was threatened. Denise has been in prison for a week and had absolutely no threats at all. Even the guards seemed to act as if she was in the wrong place. They never glared at her quite as much when she smiled or laughed. But if any of the rest of us showed any ounce of enjoyment, they act as if we were up to something suspicious.

I had learned to ignore a lot of things in my first few months of prison and continued to try and make the best of my situation. Every night when I went to sleep, I knew that I had no regrets about the crime I committed and that I would have done it again. I wouldn't have changed a thing, except for how long it took me to commit my crime and the fact that I had been caught.

I had found where Wesley had run off to the first night I went looking for him. Fortunately for me, his younger brother spilled the beans by saying that he was heading for Peoria. I ended up arriving in Peoria by the next morning. With only two thousand people in total population, I figured I'd find him quickly, kill him and be home by the next day. That wasn't exactly the case as I was soon to find out.

Once I was in Peoria, I waited until night and then went to the local bars where I figured he'd be hanging out. I didn't see him anywhere. There weren't many bars of course in such a small town and I had gone to every one of them. I sat down at a table at one of the bars and before long the waitress came over with a drink I hadn't ordered. I had ordered one beer and was only about halfway through but she was bringing another one already. She then explained that the man at the bar had purchased it for me. I figured I'd take it and then ask him about Wesley.

Taking the beer worked as far as getting him to my table but once I asked about Wesley, he replied, "I haven't seen your 'boyfriend'. Never mind. Just don't take the beer then if you're not interested." I had offended him by mistake but it gave me an idea. I began going to the different bars and introducing myself as Detective Snyder. It amazed me at how quickly people straightened up and responded properly when they thought they were speaking with a Detective.

The first few bars I went to didn't give me any leads at all. No one had even heard of Wesley. I went to a few more throughout the night and finally met a man who had information. The man told me he had worked with Wesley.

I was relieved to hear that he had some information to give me so I sat down and began asking more questions. "Can you tell me where I can find him?" "Uh, the last I knew, he was working down at the garage on Fifth Street. But, he usually comes here every Friday and Saturday night and he ain't here tonight. Not sure where he might be."

I asked around a little more but that was the extent of the information I was going to get. I walked down the road until I found a motel to stay in for the night. At least I knew where he was working. Perhaps he wasn't feeling well enough to go out for some drinks. I planned to pay a visit to the garage the next day.

When I went to the garage, I saw a couple of mechanics working on cars and I nonchalantly looked around for Wesley. I didn't see him anywhere but figured he may be out of site or on a break. An older mechanic came out and asked, "Can I help you, Miss?"

"I hope so. I'm looking for Wesley Strand. Is he here?" I said as calmly as I could. He responded, "No, but if you do see that son of a bitch, he owes me credits. Last I heard he was going away for a week to visit family in El Dorado but I haven't seen him since. That was over two weeks ago. I gave him an advance on his pay for the week just before he left."

I had to figure out where El Dorado was. I had never heard of it. I asked, "Do you know where El Dorado is?" "Yup, it's somewhere south of here in Arkansas." My heart sunk. I had a few more credits but not nearly enough to get to Arkansas. I had to come up with a new plan. I then asked him, "Are you hiring anyone right now? I have experience with a scanner and register. I worked at a convenient store before I moved."

He looked at me in disbelief at his luck as he replied, "I need to replace Wesley. That's the job I had him doing. But I can promise you that if you ask me for an advance on your credits, the answers gonna be no." I figured that much and agreed. He told me to be back the next day to start. I had just enough credits to pay for my room and buy food until the end of the week.

I stayed in Peoria for just over six months in order to save enough credits to buy a bus ticket to El Dorado. The boss at the garage had a small apartment available in back of the store. He let me stay there rent free during my time in Peoria. I stole food from the store just as I had done back home. This allowed me to save more of my credits for the trip to El Dorado. I wondered if Wesley actually did have family in El Dorado and how I would get him alone long enough to carry out my plan. I obviously couldn't kill him in front of other people, especially his family.

However, working in a convenient store in a small town gave me plenty of time to think about how I would approach the situation. My main concern was whether or not Wesley would still be in El Dorado once I arrived. I figured he would be since he had probably moved in with family and was settled into a better job. I felt I had enough time to earn the credits and perfect my plan.

It had been another long day in prison. Wake up and eat a meal. Sit outside and then eat again. Work, then back upstairs to eat dinner. As I walked into the cafeteria I noticed right away that the atmosphere seemed strange to me. It wasn't as chaotic as it normally was with prisoners rushing around trying to find their seats. As I observed my surroundings, I noticed that many of the inmates were looking toward my direction as if they were bracing themselves for something horrible to happen right in front of their eyes.

Then, I saw Jaye standing at the end of the food line. She was also staring over toward me. She then dropped her tray and began to wave her arms wildly as she started walking toward me. I was confused by this. Before I could question what was going on, I felt an intense pain across the left side of my face. It was so intense that it knocked me off my feet.

Before I could respond or even know what hit me, I was falling to the floor. I put my arms out and braced myself for impact. Seconds after I had hit the floor, I bounced back up again and looked around for the person who had caught me off guard. That's when I saw her. Shelly. She was standing directly in front of me by this point with fists raised, ready to pounce.

I attacked. I remembered the last fight I was in and kept telling myself to just start swinging. We were about the same size but Shelly was much stronger than me. I had a chance with my speed and intelligence but she outweighed me by a lot with her muscles. I swung and hit her in the head. She felt it. I saw her shaking it off just before I felt a punch to the stomach. She knocked the wind out of me but I couldn't let her have the satisfaction of knowing it. I continued swinging and got a few more punches in. She got a few also.

I was swinging wildly and trying desperately to remain standing after each blow to the head, stomach and anywhere else she could get a good hit in. We were practically on top of each other and I couldn't tell who was winning at this point. I knew I was hitting her because my knuckles were beginning to ache a little. I knew she was hitting me because I could feel the intense pain in my body. My adrenaline was the only thing keeping me from falling to the floor.

I could hear the other inmates as they were shouting and yelling. I couldn't tell who they were cheering for. I was afraid of what the other drug girls would do to me if I did win. Suddenly, I realized that I was in trouble whether I win or not. If I win, Shelly's friends would come after me and I'd still be watching my back at every corner just waiting for another fight. If I lose, who's to say that other inmates wouldn't see me as an easy target and try to pick a fight with me just to show off to their respected gangs?

Then, Shelly grabbed my hair on both sides and started pushing me toward the wall. I could feel her strength as I desperately tried to stand my ground but failed. All I could think about was Jaye's old friend Mary. I tried to stop but as she pushed with all her body weight, I couldn't. I knew what she was about to do. I was headed for the wall and she had a tight grip on me. She was going to try and kill me by hitting my head against the wall as hard as she could and I could do little to control my fate.

Where were the guards? They responded quickly in the courtyard. Plus, they had reassigned Shelly afterward. They were my only hope at this point. I tried to swing but the grip she had on me also seemed to block her face and body from being hit. She was a professional at this and I was about to lose. I felt another intense pain but this time on the back of my head as she slammed me against the wall. She pulled my head forward and slammed it backward again and I felt as if I would lose consciousness with one more blow.

I felt dizzy and went weak in the legs. I couldn't stand up. As she let go of my head, I fell to the ground. I was still conscious and actually wondered why she had let go. Why hadn't she continued banging my head against the wall until I was unconscious? She must have known that I wasn't going to die from a couple of hits to the back of the head. She obviously knew what she was doing.

As I fell to the ground, I looked back at Shelly and realized why she had let me go. It wasn't her choice to do so. As I laid on the ground only moments after falling, I noticed that her entire body was convulsing. She was staring straight ahead as she also fell to the ground in some sort of seizure. Then, I saw the dart sticking out of her back. She had been shot by a Tazer Dart. The fight was over and the guards came running in to break it up.

Even though I knew I was going to spend some time in solitary confinement for this, I was glad they had reacted when they did. If the guards hadn't of shot her with the dart, she would have killed me. I saw Jaye as the guards were picking me up off the floor and dragging me away. She just stood there looking relieved that it was over.

"Where are you taking me?" I asked. But the two guards didn't answer. They just took me out of the cafeteria and down a long corridor to the front entrance of the prison. I noticed that the corridor was dark and there weren't any guards in this area besides the two that were escorting me. I knew that solitary was in the other direction and was confused as to where we were going.

I then remembered that Jaye had told me about the policy after a fight breaks out. First, they take the prisoner's to the hospital for the Nurse to check them out. Then, they put the prisoner in solitary for up to one week. I realized in that moment that I was going to the hospital. I was relieved once I realized this and stopped fighting the guards immediately. It was probably a good idea to have a Nurse check my wounds to be sure I wouldn't end up as Mary had six months earlier.

I knew that the island had its own hospital area for the prisoner's but I had no idea where it was. In fact, until this point I hadn't given it much thought. We walked down the corridor until we came to a closed door that had 'Visitor's Area' written across the front of it.

We then turned right to go down another small hallway and around to the front entrance of the main building. Once we were at the front entrance, one of the guards put shackles on me and the other said, "Don't try anything." What was I going to do? Run? I remained quiet and simply nodded to reassure him that I wouldn't try to escape.

We walked outside, down a few steps and to the left toward another building. It was a small building compared to the actual prison but looked as if it may be large enough to keep some equipment on hand for examining a prisoner if they were seriously injured. There were other buildings around the prison that I could see well in daylight. Just past the hospital, there were about three other buildings that looked much like homes and the ocean was just beyond that. When I had been brought to the island originally, it was dark and I hadn't really observed the area well.

Once we were inside the hospital, I noticed that it was very clean and quiet compared to the prison. A Nurse came out from the back area right away and instructed the guards to put me in one of the rooms. We walked past the front counter and went into one of the three examination rooms just behind that. They took the shackles and converted them into cuffs by taking the cuff from my left ankle and my right arm and clicking them closed on the bars that were attacked to the frame of the chair I sat in. That kept me restrained to the chair itself.

As we waited for the Nurse, we all sat there in silence. I could hear a little commotion outside of the room through the closed door. I listened carefully to what was happening and recognize Shelly's voice right away. She was yelling back at the guards as they were taking her to one of the examination rooms to be checked by the Nurse.

As I waited there with the guards that had escorted me, I observed the room around me and all of the equipment. The chair was directly in the middle of the room with counter tops along the walls on both sides. The counter tops were lined with syringes, needles and other small supplies that would normally be in an examination room.

On the right side, there was a cupboard above the counter with a lock on each door. The doors had glass on the front and I could somewhat see the contents inside. I saw small vials lined up. They were each labeled. Some of the vials contained Morphine while others contained Dilaudid. I knew both of these items were strong narcotics and could understand why they would be under lock and key.

To my left, there were cupboards with glass doors but no locks. I could see the contents inside the glass doors but I really didn't know what they all meant. There were bottles lined up inside of these cupboards. Some of the bottles had the labels Propofol and Versed while others had the labels Lidocaine 2% and Zofran. I figured that these drugs must not have been as valuable for someone to possibly steal since they weren't locked up.

Above me there was a bright light that could be moved away from the wall in different directions depending on what type of lighting the Nurse needed. There was also an intercom on the wall that had a single button below it with the word 'emergency' printed just underneath of it. I wasn't sure why they would need an emergency button since prisoners are restrained during an exam. I figured it must have been in case the actual prisoner was in some sort of an emergency situation such as bleeding out, unconscious or a heart attack.

The Nurse came in and held a pen light in front of my face while instructing me to follow it with my eyes. She moved it up and down and side to side. I must have passed the test because we were quickly on to the next. She turned out the bright light overhead and shone a small light into each eye.

She turned the lights back on and began asking questions, "Can you tell me your name?" I answered correctly. "Do you feel dizzy?" I said no. She then turned to the guards and said, "I think she's going to be fine. No need for a brain scan." At that, they converted the cuffs back into shackles and led me back to the prison building, down the corridor and straight to solitary confinement.

Shelly had won and I was being punished. Of course, I was certain that she was in a cell nearby being punished as well. I wondered to myself if the exam was thorough enough. It didn't seem to me that it was.

I was afraid that I would end up like Jaye's friend Mary and not wake up the next morning. My head continued to throb and no one ever offered any medication to help. I didn't even get the chance to ask for anything. Despite the pain and the fear of not waking up, I went to sleep.

# Chapter 10
# Solitary Confinement

I woke up to the sound of the small window to the door of my cell sliding open and a breakfast tray being pushed through. The guard on the other side of the door said, "Breakfast. Eat up. Shower time is in one hour." I was confused. I didn't realize I was going to be granted the privilege of taking a shower while in this cell. When I had first arrived, I was put in solitaire and wasn't given any time at all outside of the small eight by eight cell.

I grabbed my tray and began eating the cold eggs and stale toast. I wasn't sure what I was supposed to do before showers since this was my first day. In my usual cell, I was expected to clean and get dressed but in my new temporary cell, there wasn't anything for me to clean.

The room only consisted of a mattress laid against one wall, a toilet in the corner and a small light in the other corner. The room was rather dim compared to the rest of the prison, which made it difficult to see. I knew that reading or writing was not going to be an option.

I had no idea how I would possibly keep myself busy for an

entire week but I had managed before when I was first brought to Clausdrum. I figured I would do the same as I did then, which was sleep most of the time. I thought that would make the week go by much more quickly.

Once an hour had passed by, the guard opened the door to my cell and the light from the hallway flooded in without warning. I was blinded for a moment and shielded my eyes from the bright light. He yelled, "Get up! It's time for a shower." As I stood up and walked over to the doorway of my cell, I noticed that the other doors were being opened as the rest of the inmates were being told the same. I noticed that the solitary cells were located in the same row as Cell Block D.

The women of Cell Block D were much tougher looking than the others. They didn't talk to each other much and seemed a little more insane. There were also a few other women from the solitary cells, including the women who had tried to escape and Shelly. I tried my best to keep my distance. Shelly looked like she had been through a war so I figured she hadn't gotten much sleep the night before.

We lined up as we were told and marched down to the shower area. As I walked past the cells of Cell Block D, I made a point to look inside one of them to see how the other half live. Apparently, the Cell Block D women did get a brighter light than I had in my solitary cell, but their cells were slightly smaller than my regular cell.

They were all furnished the same as the cells in the general population with a table, chair, bed and toilet. The only difference other than the size was the door to the cells. They had large steel doors with a slit in the front for passing trays of food just like the solitary cells. From inside their cells, they couldn't tell if it was day or night.

The process of shower time was essentially the same except a little less crowed. So, instead of taking shifts to the shower area, we all went in at the same time. The total number of women, including solitary and Cell Block D, was approximately thirty. We washed up in silence as everyone looked straight ahead. The guards seemed to be stricter than the guards that work with the general population. I figured that no one spoke to each other because they were afraid to.

They gave me only a clean yellow jumpsuit with my number on it as a change of clothing. I didn't get pajamas like I did in my regular area and I suddenly felt that I had been slightly spoiled by that. However, I did notice that the women of Cell Block D did get a pair to take to their rooms. I paid close attention to make sure that they just didn't forget mine but noticed right away that Shelly and the other women from the solitary cells didn't receive pajamas either. I assumed that wasn't a privilege we would receive while we were being punished.

Once we were clean and dressed, we were sent back upstairs to our cells and the guards yelled as if they were herding cattle. Just as I entered my cell, I turned around to see a guard facing me about two inches from my face. He looked familiar and he stated, "Remember me?" It took me a few moments but I eventually did. This was the guard I had spit on when I first arrived. He had given me quite a beating with his night stick.

"I do remember you from my first night here." I replied. "Glad to see I made an impression." He growled back. "We're not going to have any problems with you, are we?" He asked as he waved his night stick in my direction. I shook my head and avoided eye contact. "Good. That's what I thought. I'll be paying close attention."

He walked out and slammed the door. I laid down on my mattress and tried to go to sleep. No matter how hard I tried, I couldn't. I just wasn't tired enough to force myself to drift off. It wasn't even lunch time on my first day and I already felt that I could easily lose my mind in this place.

What could I possibly do for an entire week with only four plain walls to look at? I had my three meals and thought maybe I could make them last all the way until the next meal was served but I was too hungry by the time I was given something to eat.

I sat there with only my thoughts and the only thing I could think about was my freedom. I longed to be free again and to make my own choices. I longed to be able to live my life without the restraints of someone telling me what to do, what to eat and how to act all the time. I didn't want to have to look over my shoulder constantly wondering when I was going to be attacked. If I wasn't being yelled at by a guard, I was being physically or verbally attacked by another prisoner.

Prior to killing Wesley, I had gotten the opportunity to travel. I had gone to Peoria and then headed south to El Dorado. I had worked for six months in Peoria before I finally had enough credits to go to El Dorado. The only thing I wished I could have changed was the fact that I was so focused on finding Wesley that I forgot to enjoy myself. I really didn't make any friends in the places I had been. I only asked people if they knew Wesley and spent the rest of the time thinking of how I was going to kill him.

The owner of the garage I worked at let me stay in a small area just behind the garage. I wondered if Wesley had stayed in the same room at one point but I never asked. I didn't earn many credits for the job I did. So, I stole the necessities and saved the credits for my next venture. I was a natural for stealing what I needed and never got caught. I stole food and clothing mostly. Occasionally, I stole other items such as movies to try and take my mind off of Wesley for a short time, but my thoughts always returned to him.

After I had worked for nearly six months in Peoria, I quit my job and headed for El Dorado, which was yet another small town. There were more people in El Dorado than there were in Peoria, but it was still small by most standards. There were less than twenty thousand people in the town and in the surrounding areas.

As soon as I arrived in El Dorado, I did the same thing I had done in Peoria. Upon my arrival, I went to the local bars and clubs and asked around. Again, I introduced myself as Detective Snyder and people responded rather well and gave any information they had. There were a few that asked to see a badge so I had to lie and say I wasn't carrying it because I was off duty. They didn't buy my story on that and I got no information from them.

There were a few people that were too drunk to think to ask for a badge and, luckily, they had information. They had said that Wesley's girlfriend had family in the area and that they had been staying with them for quite a while. Wesley had been working at her uncle's welding business and was learning the trade. I got the name of the business and planned on a visit the next day.

The business was a small welding company located in an industrial park. They used the garage in the back of the building for most of their work. I walked up and asked the first person I saw if they knew Wesley.

As soon as I had asked, an older man came out from behind some heavy equipment and started shouting while shaking his fists, "You know that son of a bitch, Wesley? You tell your friend that if I get my hands on him..." He didn't finish his sentence but I could fill in the rest. "He's not a friend." I stopped myself because I realized it wouldn't be a good idea to say that I was a detective. These men were sober and would probably ask for identification, which I didn't have.

I continued, "I'm not really a friend. I only know him from high school..." I was stuttering to come up with something they would believe. Fortunately, the old man didn't care much about why I wanted to find him. He interrupted, "Look, I don't care why you want to find him. He's dating my niece and I tried to help him out by giving him a job. All he did was complain all day about doing a little hard labor. I'm old school and I finally said something. Well, he's just too hot headed for me I guess and ran out leaving us with all this work. As far as I heard he was heading out to California to find a better job."

I asked if he knew what part of California but he didn't. He even went as far as making a few phone calls on my behalf to other family members who may know his exact whereabouts. Every time he hung up the phone, he would shake his head. My heart sank each time. He finally made a phone to one last relative that may have possibly known where Wesley was heading when he left.

As I stood there listening to his conversation, I became a little excited, "You do? Oh that's great. There's someone here that's looking for him." He paused and then continued in a slightly softer voice, "I'm thinking he probably owes credits."

After a few more minutes, he thanked the person on the other end and hung up. He looked at me and said, "I know where you can find him. He went to San Francisco." My hopes were high in that moment. I was going to find Wesley Strand.

On the other hand, I didn't have nearly enough credits to get there. I went back to the motel room I was staying in and tried to come up with another plan. By this point, I had been in El Dorado for just over a week and I was already running low on credits. I wasn't about to go home defeated by this mission. I was going to find Wesley no matter what it took. I decided that the next day, I would look for another temporary job and eventually buy a ticket to California.

As I sat in my cell remembering back to my hunt for Wesley, the window to the door opened and a lunch try was pushed through. They served a plate of wilted salad and a ham sandwich on stale bread. I was hungry enough that I didn't care anymore. After being in prison for quite a while, I had gotten used to the meals and was usually hungry enough by the time I did get to eat that I hardly even noticed the stale bread.

I began thinking more about the adventure I had been on prior to my incarceration. After I had worked for ten months in El Dorado at a convenient store, stole food from local stores and saved enough credits to head out to California, I bought my ticket to San Francisco. I was ready to meet up with Wesley and make him pay for what he did. If he could take my sister's life then I could take his. I felt that I had a valid reason for my mission.

Once I arrived in San Francisco, I was taken aback by the amount of people in this one city. It was extremely crowded. My home town wasn't nearly as small as Peoria and probably bigger than El Dorado but I had never seen a place that was this populated. There were big screens on the corner of buildings with advertisements playing all the time.

The people would just brush past you without even smiling or acknowledging your existence. The streets were packed with cars all traveling at high speeds and there were a few strange looking trains that looked as if they were missing the front half. They shared the road with the rest of the traffic but stopped frequently. I realized right away that they were strange looking buses.

There were a lot of hills compared to the city I had just come from and the homes were mostly row homes. I didn't even know where to go from the bus station. I just started walking. Eventually I came to a motel and checked in for the night. I had trouble sleeping the first night because of the noise level in the streets. It never stopped. However, it did quiet down just a little at about four in the morning, which was when I finally drifted off to sleep.

The next morning I woke up to the noise of traffic and people coming and going once again. I had to reorient myself on where I was. Once I had gotten up and dressed for the day, I went out to look for a job. It was a little harder than I had anticipated. In the other two towns I had just been in, I was given a job almost immediately. However, it just seemed impossible in San Francisco.

Several of the owner's in the convenient stores snapped, "No! We're not hiring." They weren't friendly at all.

I had always heard that many years ago, San Francisco was a friendly place to live and everyone was cheerful and excepting of new people. Over the last few decades, with the economy crashing several times, things had changed. San Francisco was very busy, unfriendly and expensive.

There were a lot of homeless people in the streets with no shoes or socks begging for food. They sat there with an emaciated appearance as they clung tightly to signs with the writing, "Homeless, please give me food and water." I saw other people standing nearby in the streets with signs as well but their signs had the words, "The End is Near, Repent."

Eventually, after a few days of searching, I did get hired at a restaurant. It wasn't much of one and all they served was pizza, but it was a nice family friendly type of place. I was hired as a hostess where my job was to simply find a seat for families coming in. It was easy enough but the pay was horrible. I realized that I wouldn't be able to live in a motel with the pay I was receiving. I knew it would take a long time to find Wesley in a place this large and this would be my home until I was successful at what I came here to do.

I found a small basement to rent from a woman who was only charging two hundred credits per month. She had several other apartments in the building but the one she rented to me was the cheapest. She also gave me the option to rent month to month so that I wouldn't be locked in to a long term lease. I was just glad to have a place to sleep each night that was within my budget.

On the nights that I wasn't working, I spent time going to local bars and once again asking if anyone had heard of Wesley. It was much harder to find anyone with information in a large city but I was determined to keep trying. It got to the point where I began asking people everywhere I went. I even asked people in the streets at times. Most people didn't want to be bothered and the rest of them had no information at all. I was beginning to get desperate and believing that I was going to fail at finding him.

I had spent almost a year in San Francisco before my luck finally changed. One night I was at a local bar about to give up when a man about my age sat down next to me. He asked why I looked so depressed and if there was anything he could do to cheer me up. I said, "Not unless you can tell me where Wesley Strand is hiding."

"Actually, I can point you in the right direction but can't say exactly where he ran off to." This was the most information I had gotten from anyone in almost a year. I couldn't believe that I had finally found someone who recognized the name. I verified it was the right person by asking him about our hometown and high school. It was definitely the Wesley Strand that I was after. I was excited as I asked, "How do you know him? Where is he?"

The man laughed and said, "He's south of here somewhere now. But before that, he moved out here a while ago and we kept in touch. He kept bragging about how awesome this place was and told me I should move out here too. He had a good job and there was room for more employees. He was a contractor in construction. I jumped at the opportunity and moved out here to take a job at the company he was working for." I asked, "So, where is he now? Do you know where he lives?"

He shook his head and continued, "It was me, him and his girlfriend until he decided he didn't like the weather here in the winter time. He moved to Florida but I'm not sure which part. Maybe Orlando. Actually, it was Orlando now that I'm thinking about it. We lost touch over the last several months since he left. I'm not much for jumping around and I make pretty good money so I stayed here."

That night, I did some calculations and research on how many credits I would need in order to get to Florida and found that

101

I would have to work for another six months before I would finally have enough. Patience was not something I was lacking in as long as I knew I would find him eventually. I stole enough food and other needed supplies, which enabled me to only have to work for another five months before heading off to Florida.

As I stared at one of the walls in my prison cell and wondered if I'd ever get to sleep, my dinner tray was pushed through the small opening in the door, the guard said, "Another hour and you get to go outside. Enjoy." I was surprised to hear that I would actually get to go outside. I figured we would be taken to the courtyard and I was nervous about spending time with the people in this area of the prison.

All the women of Cell Block D were more withdrawn and heavily supervised compared the other areas. I was a little intimidated at the thought of socializing with them. Plus, I already knew I wasn't going to try and socialize with the other women in solitary, especially Shelly.

Aside from Shelly, the other women who were in solitary had just tried to escape a few weeks prior and I did not want to be associated with women who had committed such a horrible crime. I felt it was too risky so I decided that I would stay to myself during our free time in the courtyard.

During the time I had traveled, I had taken for granted the free time I had. I could have enjoyed the sites and the places I had been. Maybe I would have if I had known I would spend the rest of my life behind bars and heavy doors. For the first time since my arrival to Clausdrum, I began to regret the crime I had committed. Then, I realized I wasn't regretting the crime as much as I was regretting the fact that I had been caught.

I realized that there was no going back in time and that I would eventually die in this place. I began getting depressed as I sat alone in solitary confinement and my first day wasn't even over yet. I had at least six more days to go before I would be allowed to be with other inmates. I wasn't sure if I was going to make it through the week. I had to force myself to sleep if I was going to survive.

# Chapter 11
# Cell Block D

To my relief, the door opened again a little while after dinner had been served and a guard standing outside of my cell instructed us all to line up for the courtyard. We all marched in the direction that led to the outside, through the doorway and into the fresh air. We had two hours to spend outside before being herded back into our cells again. I was just glad to be out of the dark cell and into the open air again.

As soon as we were outside, I watched the inmates to see where they were going to sit and congregate. It didn't seem as organized with different groups congregating together as it was in the general population. The women from Cell Block D just stood around and sat in different places and kept to themselves.

They didn't even really make eye contact with each other. A few of them were smoking their cigarettes as they were lost in their thoughts while others just looked out beyond the fenced in area daydreaming about another life. I found a place to sit at a picnic table that was close to the building. It was a cold day and with the sun setting, the coldness of the air was even more noticeable.

Shortly after I had sat down, the woman sitting beside me said, "Are you new here?" "Sort of. I've been at the prison for about six months. I'm spending time in solitary. Apparently, fighting with other inmates gets you an upgrade to the dark cell." She laughed at my comment and said, "I'm Dolores. I got an upgrade to a permanent dark cell. I'm on Cell Block D."

I was a little nervous talking with someone from Cell Block D since I had heard that most of these prisoners were extremely dangerous. I had been told that they are too dangerous to be integrated with the general population. Dolores seemed very gruff in the way that she spoke but she certainly didn't come across as dangerous. She was a middle aged women with gray hair and very thin.

As she smoked her cigarette she continued the conversation with me. "So, what are you in here for?" "I killed a man out of revenge." She smiled and then asked, "So, how did you do it?" She seemed intrigued and almost entertained by murder. I wasn't sure if I should respond to that or not.

Fortunately another woman intervened and said, "Dolores, leave the new kid alone." Dolores got up and walked away as if she were a child being told to leave the room. The other woman was sitting across from me at the picnic table. She was a younger woman, maybe in her thirties. She had long brown hair and was built very muscular.

"Don't mind Dolores, she's harmless." She paused as if considering her own comment and corrected herself, "Well, she's not really harmless. She's dangerous. Killed twenty two people before the police got her. And for no good reason at all." I was glad that this new person showed up but was a little less than trusting at this point. I only nodded and smiled at her comment about the other inmate.

She continued anyway, "I'm Megan. I was in the general population before. I tried to escape a few years back and when I didn't succeed, they put me here." I looked over and saw the four women who had attempted to escape just a few weeks ago and

105

wondered if they would also end up in Cell Block D after their time in solitary.

Megan must have notice and said, "Most people don't end up in Cell Block D when they try to escape. Those four women over there will serve their time and move back to their old cells." I asked, "So, why did you end up here permanently?" "Well, it's complicated. When I first arrived to the prison, they weren't sure if I was Cell Block D worthy at that point. They were on the fence from the beginning on where to put me. They probably flipped a coin over it or something but, either way, I ended up in a regular cell at first."

That made sense to me. I was guessing that her escape was the deciding factor in putting her in Cell Block D. She continued to explain, "When they caught me trying to escape, they figured I was too dangerous and hard to control. The Warden made an executive decision to move me here and I've been here ever since." Her story seemed to make sense to me and I could understand why she ended up in Cell Block D. I nodded to let her know this.

"Most of the women over on this side don't talk much. And when they do, don't answer them." She said. Then she leaned in and softened her voice, "They're crazy over here." I could tell that she wasn't playing with a full deck either. She seemed to fit right in with the rest of the women in this area. I had no question about that. It was almost like being in a prison with several inmates like Crazy Chris.

Then I wondered why Crazy Chris wasn't in Cell Block D. Her crime was rather horrific and she was definitely crazy, hence the nickname. I figured it may have been because of her innocent childlike craziness. Perhaps they felt it would be too dangerous for her to be with these women. She was obviously influenced easily and these women would recognize that immediately.

After witnessing four women attempt to escape only a few weeks ago and knowing their plan, at least partially, I was curious to know how Megan had tried to escape. I wasn't sure how she would respond but I asked anyway, "What was your plan?" She leaned in to speak to me and watched every guard carefully to make sure they weren't listening as she spoke to me about it. I didn't blame her for being cautious. It seemed to be a touchy subject and I certainly didn't want to get into trouble or even draw attention to myself for talking to someone about their escape plan.

"I had dish duty in the afternoons. I watched the guards on a regular basis and found that they had a simple routine. My plan was to find an escape route that wasn't very heavily guarded, overtake a guard so that I could take his Tazer Dart gun. Then, take one of the floaters they have lined up outside. I figured once I got to the other side, I'd ditch my microchip and live off the land."

I was beginning to realize that Megan was just as crazy as the rest of the women on this side of the prison. I asked, "So, how far did you get?" She looked around a little to make sure no one was listening and said, "Well, during dish duty I took one of the pairing knives and killed the inmate that was working with me. Stabbed her right in the jugular."

I was shocked but kept listening. "Then, when the guard came over to see what was going on, I punched him in the stomach and managed to get his Tazer gun. He wasn't expecting it. You see, it's all about the element of surprise. You get people to trust you and then wham!" She laughed at her own comment and continued, "Once I had the Tazer gun in my own hands, I ran as fast as I could out into the courtyard. Then, I ran up the bleachers and scaled the fence."

I asked, "Weren't the guards after you by this point?" "Oh, yes," she continued, "and I shot at least three of them with the Tazer gun on my way through the courtyard. The gun was loaded with at least six rounds. All of them are. Everyone knows that." She said this as if I should know all about Tazer guns. I didn't.

I only knew that they contained small darts that have

enough electricity to stun a person for about twenty seconds. They release the electricity on impact. This allows the guards to shoot from a distance of at least thirty feet, depending on how good their aim is of course. Then, the guards have twenty seconds to come up on the prisoner where they can easily detain them once the electricity has finished coursing through the prisoner's body.

She continued with her story, "I got just on the other side of the fence when I was finally caught." She looked as if this were the only part of her plan that she regretted. "They brought me back in, put me in solitary confinement for about two weeks before they finally decided to make this a permanent home for me."

"What happened to the woman you had stabbed." I inquired. "Well, she died. I stabbed her right in the neck. They didn't get to her quick enough to save her. She bled out in minutes." She said this with absolutely no compassion at all. She spoke about killing the person as if she were talking about what she had for dinner the night before.

I knew this woman was insane and made it a point to talk as little as possible with her from that moment on. She was a psychopath and it was obvious after only hearing her speak for about ten minutes. I didn't want to piss her off either so I continued to listen to her speak and gave her only limited information about myself when she had asked.

She did tell me a little about the other inmates of Cell Block D. There was Stacey who had committed several homicides with no reason at all. Apparently, she had some kind of disorder where she would begin to mimic someone she envied. Then, she would start stalking that person but would keep her distance enough so that the person really couldn't do anything about it. She would start to look like her next victim by dressing like the person and changing her hair to look just like theirs.

Eventually, she would kill the person and no one really knew why. Megan had explained that there was a psychiatrist that came to the island a couple of times per month to work with the women of Cell Block D. He basically talks with the inmates and then reports his findings and opinions on whether or not they should ever be released to the general population. Stacey had been in Cell Block D for twenty years. She was one of the first inmates to Clausdrum.

There was another inmate that Megan pointed out to me that had murdered at least twenty five men. She had been a prostitute since she was about sixteen. Eventually, she began killing the men. She would take them to a remote location, kill them and take their microchip. Apparently, she had an accomplice that would wire the credits to another account. She did this for almost twelve years before anyone caught on to her scheme.

As I sat outside each day with Megan, she told me more stories about the inmates of Cell Block D and why they were kept under such close watch. After hearing what they had done, I appreciated the fact that they were kept isolated from the rest of the prisoners. I couldn't even begin to imagine what it would be like if they were among the rest of us.

Megan had pointed out prisoners that were serial killers and would kill a person just because someone looked a certain way. For example, there was one prisoner that had killed almost forty people in her day simple because of their age and appearance. The psychiatrist had reported that she probably knew someone in her past that fit this description but had yet to find out why she had so much hatred toward that person.

Another woman supposedly had multiple personalities. She had been diagnosed with almost forty of them. Her crime was assault and battery that would quickly lead to murder depending on the personality that was present at that time. She could be a sweet woman one second and suddenly turn on a person and be murderous the next. She had killed several people at random prior to being caught.

I wasn't too thrilled about hearing what these women were capable of. However, it did pass the time rather well during my time in solitary. It also helped to ease my nervousness since I knew I had someone to talk to during the courtyard time. Knowing how dangerous these women were made me realize how unsafe the environment was and I took extra precautions during my time outside of the dark cell.

Megan was dangerous as well and I was intimidated by her, but she didn't seem to be a threat toward me. I sat on the opposite side of the picnic table while she spoke to me and watched her like a hawk. I didn't want to end up stabbed like her co-worker had been and I didn't trust that she wasn't going to do something crazy again. All she needed was the right opportunity to make a move on an innocent person.

There were more guards watching over us and that did make me feel a little safer, but I still kept my distance. Once we would go back to our cells, I did manage to sleep often. I suppose I had just been too nervous the first day to get any rest at all, but by the second day, I was sleeping in between meals with no problem.

When I wasn't asleep, I thought more about the time I had spent traveling the country in search for Wesley. Once I was on my way to Florida, I thought more about how I would approach the situation once I found him. At least I knew he wasn't living with family in Florida and the only person I had to watch out for was his girlfriend.

I wasn't sure who his girlfriend was at that time, but I knew I'd have to stalk Wesley for a certain amount of time anyway and would soon learn her identity. Once I found him, I'd have to watch his every move to learn his schedule and routine. I had to know when he would be alone and for how long.

I still wasn't sure how I was going to carry out the crime, but I did know that he would be dead soon enough. I couldn't wait to see the look on his face upon seeing me and felt a little excited about the event. I was getting slightly anxious as well about finding him and carrying out my mission. He was much bigger than I was and I had no weapon to my name.

I figured I'd find him first and then while stalking him I'd figure out how to kill him. I was determined enough to come up with a way to carry out this plan. The thought of making sure he paid for what he had done to my sister was enough to keep me going.

I arrived in Florida by plane and was overwhelmed once again by the enormity of yet another city. It was a large city with many buildings and people everywhere. The buildings weren't quite as tall as the buildings in San Francisco and there were no advertisements scrolling by. I was slightly relieved to see that the people were a little friendlier in Orlando as well.

There was a lot of traffic just as there was in San Francisco, but the buses in Orlando looked different. They were taller and filled with families going to amusement parks in the area. There were also a lot of people walking down the streets of the city area. Once I had moved further away from where the amusement parks were located, I saw fewer families. Further into the city, there were more bars and night clubs than there were children.

I found a small place to rent once again and a job working in a factory. It was a different type of job than I had held in the past but the sign had said no experience necessary. Once I started work, I quickly realized why this was the case. I really didn't need more than a day's worth of training to perform my new job. My only responsibility was to empty boxes by placing the items on shelves and breaking down the boxes.

The job was much busier than my previous jobs and I had less time to think about my mission. I did find time in the evenings when I wasn't working and spent much of my free time going to bars as I had done in the other cities. I continued to ask people if they had heard of Wesley Strand and most of the people hadn't.

I figured if I had found someone with information in a city as large as San Francisco, than I would definitely find him in Orlando. I never gave up. I knew he had been doing construction jobs previously so I came up with an idea to go to different construction sites and look for him there.

The only problem I had with this at first was the fact that my job was Monday through Friday and during the day. So, by the time I left my job, most of the construction sites were deserted for the day. I wasn't having much luck with finding him. I had to come up with a way around my dilemma so I spoke with my new boss.

I requested a night shift position at the factory but was told there were no openings at the time. My boss had said, "As soon as something opens up, I can switch you over to the night shift." I agreed and figured I'd continue with what I had been doing so far in my search. After about six months, there was finally a shift open for the nights and I switched immediately.

After I had moved to the night shift, I quickly got a new routine that worked well with my search for Wesley. I would go in at eleven at night and get off at seven in the morning. Once I left work, I would spend the rest of the morning going to different construction sites asking people if they knew Wesley.

I did this for another six months when my luck changed one morning. I had left work as usual and went to a couple of construction sites. I was told at the first two sites that no one had ever heard of Wesley. I was going to quit for the day and go home early. I was tired and my hopes were down as I thought I'd never find him. But, I told myself I'd go to one more site and then give up.

I arrived at the next site, and as I walked up to the outskirts of the fence that surrounded the area where men were working everywhere, I saw him. Wesley was on the site with his hard hat on, carrying wood across the dirt area to another worker. I froze as

112

I studied him to be sure it was Wesley.

He looked over and saw me watching him. At that moment, he dropped the wood and ran. Someone must have tipped him off that I had been on his trail. I assumed it was his old friend from San Francisco. I ran alongside of the fence to catch up with him at the back area of the construction site but he was gone before I had gotten there.

I was disappointed that I had lost him once again but at least I knew where he was. I was on the right tract and figured I'd have to find a way to tract where he was living. I showed up again the very next day and looked for him but he wasn't there. Over the next few days, I showed up and saw no sign of him. I was afraid that I had lost his trail once again.

# Chapter 12
# The Hunt Continues

For the remainder of my time in solitary, I continued to sleep as much as possible and spent the rest of the time thinking back on the days when I hunted Wesley. I felt as if I could lose my mind at any moment. Day after day, I sat in that small dark cell not knowing whether or not it was daytime or nighttime. I was beginning to feel the insanity creeping up on me and could understand how a person could easily change dramatically for the worse after spending any extended period of time in solitary confinement.

After my first couple of days, I saw that the four women who had tried to escape previously were still not released into the general population and I wondered if they ever would be. It was a total of six of us in solitary, including me and Shelly. Shelly did avoid me at every cost. In the showers, she stood at the opposite shower head from me and in the courtyard she stood by the fence while I sat at the picnic tables.

I was relieved that she kept her distance and avoided me but wondered if it was because she felt that I had won the fight or whether she was afraid of reliving these consequences. I wasn't sure but I definitely didn't feel that I had won the fight so I believed the latter of the two possibilities.

Knowing that she was doing time in solitary just like I was, I had to wonder why she seemed to be more traumatized than me. Maybe this was her last chance and her next punishment would be worse. I pondered these thoughts as I watched her from a distance.

She saw me looking a few times but she quickly looked the other way. I knew this wasn't how Shelly had been so I figured something had to have happened to change her attitude. One conclusion I had come to rather quickly after the fight was that this was not her first offense.

On the fifth day, I was awoken to my breakfast tray and then herded to the showers along with the other women. As I glanced around a little at the other women, I noticed right away that there was a new girl with us in the showers. She was a small, young woman with an innocent face and shoulder length hair. She looked familiar but I couldn't place it at first.

When I went back to my cell, I thought more about her and where I had seen her before. Then, I realized where I knew her from. She was one of the women who always stood by the fence in the courtyard. She was on afternoon shift work like me and had courtyard time in the mornings. She was one of the women from the gossipers group.

I realized she must have done something to earn some time in solitary. I decided I would ask her about it during our free time in the evening. In the meantime, I couldn't even imagine what she could have done to get a punishment such as this one. The gossipers group was harmless and stayed out of trouble. No one ever bothered them much and they never caused any trouble with anyone else.

For the remainder of the day, as I waited for each tray to be delivered and courtyard time in the evening, I tried to sleep. I had slept so much during my time in solitary that I just couldn't keep my eyes closed. My mind was saying to sleep but my body was saying no. I just wasn't tired enough. I just sat there, staring straight ahead at the plain white wall in front of me.

I thought more about my time on the outside and about the chase for Wesley. After I had seen him at the construction site, I went back a few times and didn't see him again. He had seen me watching him on the first day and made a run for it. I knew his friend from San Francisco had tipped him off about me so he must have figured I was out for revenge.

After realizing he hadn't shown up for the job, I decided to ask his boss for more information. I made up a good story to tell so that I could get some information about Wesley without sounding suspicious. I knew it was a good lie and no one would suspect that I was a danger to Wesley.

Once I had gotten off work, I went back to the construction site and asked the first person I saw, "Can you tell me who's in charge?" The man pointed to a middle aged man standing in the midst of the construction site giving instructions to another worker. I continued, "Can I talk to him? I have a few questions about Wesley Strand."

The man went over and got the bosses attention. I saw them both looking toward me as the man said something to his boss. His boss nodded and the man came walking back over toward me. He said, "Just wait here. He'll be right over." I waited there patiently for about twenty minutes.

The next thing I knew, the boss came up from behind me. He must have left the construction site from the other side of the fence and came around. He said, "Hi, I'm Matt, Wesley's boss. Come with me where it's a little quieter." I followed him to a small trailer next to the construction site and went inside.

The trailer was cluttered with papers and blueprints all over the place. Matt explained as we entered, "Excuse the mess. I'm old fashioned and still like to have the actual blueprints in front of me

116

on paper. I just can't get used to the electronic type." He was a gruff type of man that looked slightly overworked and a little overweight as well.

He cleared some paperwork off of a chair and instructed me to sit down. I did and he sat on the edge of his desk. He asked, "So, do you know where Wesley is?" I was a little disappointed but not surprise by the question. I was secretly hoping that he would tell me where Wesley was but figure he would probably have no idea at this point since Wesley hadn't shown up for work in a few days.

"No, I was hoping you would know. You see, I'm his sister and I always call him every Friday. Our family is very close." He nodded and I continued, "I called as usual this past Friday and Wesley didn't answer. I figured maybe he had to run out to the store or something and would be back, so I waited. I called back again later on and still, no answer. I tried not to worry but I was starting to just a little."

I checked his expression to make sure he was buying my story. He seemed to be as he listened intently. "The next morning, I called again and he still wasn't answering. I've never been to his house before so I don't even know what kind of neighborhood he's living in. I'm just worried that something horrible has happened to him."

The boss leaned back a little in thought as he pondered what I had said. I continued with my act. "He has a friend here from work that he talks about all the time. I was hoping maybe he would know where Wesley is but I can't remember his name exactly."

I began to pretend as if I were trying to remember the name of Wesley's friend, "It was something like Frank…Fred...Foster. Wait, maybe it was Mike or Mark..."

"Oh! You must be talking about Manny." He said this as if we had both had a revelation on the name of Wesley's friend. He

117

continued, "Hey, you may be on to something. Wesley and Manny go out for drinks all the time after work. I bet he does know what happened to Wesley and where he is. Hold on just a minute. I'll go and get him."

As soon as he left I jumped up and went straight back to a filing cabinet I had been eying from the moment we had walked into the trailer. It had the words 'Employee Files' across the top draw of the cabinet. As I opened the draw and saw the files packed in so tightly together with paperwork sticking out, I mumbled to myself, "Why can't he be like everyone else and have all the files on a computer system."

I was really counting on being able to just open up a screen, get by a password protected system and obtain the information I needed. I had done that before in school and had learned how to hack into a system, bypassing anyone's password. I wasn't a professional hacker by any means and really couldn't do much more than override a password but that little knowledge I held was really valuable in school when I wanted to change my grades from time to time.

I found the file with Wesley's name on it, pulled it out and began searching through the paperwork for his home address. "Got it!" I said to myself as I put everything back in its place the best I could. I had a good memory and didn't see the need to write it down. I kept repeating it over and over a few times until it stuck in my mind.

By the time the boss came back with Manny, I was sitting in the chair once again as if I had never gotten up. "This is Wesley's friend, Manny." The boss said as Manny looked a bit confused. Manny added, "I didn't know he had a sister. He never spoke about you." I forced myself to look offended as I replied, "Well, of all the things! Did you ever think that maybe you had too many drinks to remember?"

He apologized right away and the boss intervened. "Manny

says he hasn't heard from Wesley either in a few days. I'm sorry, ma'am, I don't know what to say. But if you do find him, you can tell him he should come back and talk with me. He's one of the best men I got out there and I'm willing to give him another chance."

I cringed a little when the boss had replied this way but swallowed my anger quickly and thanked him for his time. I left the small construction trailer with high hopes. I knew where Wesley was living. He could dodge me on the job but he had to go to sleep at some point. I went back home and got a little sleep myself before having to go back to work again that night.

My cell door opened before I realized it had already been another day. I was getting used to keeping myself occupied with my thoughts throughout the day. They had already served the lunch and dinner trays and the time in between seemed to go by a little faster each day. It was now time to go outside to the courtyard.

We all lined up and began heading in that direction. I noticed that the solitary cells had seven of us now along with the usually inmates from Cell Block D. I wanted to find out more about the other woman who was in solitary and made it a point to go and talk to her once we were outside. I was too curious to pass up the opportunity to find out what she had done.

I followed her to the area near the fence about ten feet away from where Shelly was standing. When Shelly saw me, she turned around and walked toward the picnic tables. I had no idea why she was acting as if she was scared of me. I focused my thoughts back on the new woman and walked up to her.

"Hi, I'm Roxy. I've seen you before in the other area of the prison." I said. She replied, "I'm Jan. I've seen you before too. You hang with Jaye and those other women, right?" I nodded and we stood there for a few moments in silence. Finally, I asked, "So, why did you get sent over here?"

She looked back to make sure no one was nearby to hear her response. She leaned in and quietly explained, "The guards here are assholes. I work in the prison store in the afternoons and the one that supervises us is always yelling at us and making us feel stupid. I yelled back at him yesterday." I was surprised. This woman didn't look like she could yell at her own children let alone a guard. I just couldn't imagine her getting angry at another person.

The again, I could imagine how the guards could push a person to snap. They were mean and aggressive most of the time. I felt as if I could lose my control many times with the guards. However, I always assumed it was my lack of control over my own temper. I knew I had anger problems and if this woman yelled at a guard, I felt it was inevitable that I would too eventually.

As we stood there in silence for a little longer, I wanted to ask her what she knew about the other inmates. I knew she was from the gossipers group and probably had good information that I could take back to Jaye and the rest of the women. It would give us something to talk about during our courtyard time.

Finally, I asked, "So, you hang with the women that know everything that goes on in this place. Got any good information?" She smiled in a bit of a sinister way and replied, "I sure do, but you can't tell anyone you heard it from me." I agreed and listened intently as she told me the big news of the prison.

"Apparently, I got word that there's a group of women who are going to try and overtake the guards." "What do you mean by overtake them? Are they going to try and escape?" She nodded as if to say that I was catching on quickly. She continued, "I heard it's the girls from the picnic tables. Well, some of them anyway. There planning to make a break for it."

I couldn't believe what I was hearing and I commented, "After the other four women just got caught? What are they thinking?" She explained, "Well, they're theory is that most prison breaks happen after a lot of time has gone by and the guards simmer down a little. They think that this would be a good time to carry out their plan since the guards won't be expecting it. There's never been a prison break just weeks after a failed attempt by someone else."

I didn't agree with their theory at all and assumed they had spent so much time in this place that they had lost their grip on reality. I said, "Yeah, it makes sense only if you don't think about it." Jan laughed a little and continued, "I'm not sure exactly when it's going to happen but soon. They're planning on surprising the guards that stand by the entrance of Cell Block B and then take off through the front entrance to the building. I guess they'll try and swim to the mainland from there."

I added, "They'll probably take one of the floaters." Jan corrected me, "The floaters are kept on the other side of the island behind the courtyard." I smiled because I realized at that point that I had information that one of the gossipers apparently didn't have. "They keep two of them at the front of the island as well."

She looked at me with a bit of a shocked look on her face at my knowledge. "How do you know that?" She asked. I explained, "Before I was brought to this side of the prison, they took me to the hospital to get checked out. We went through the front of the building to get there. I could see the water's edge from the hospital and saw two floaters tied to the pier."

She looked back out toward the water and said, "I like you. You seem too smart to be here." That was actually the first time in my life someone had called me smart. I had never thought of myself in that way. I knew I was a survivor and could think my way through most problems, but never applied that word to the description of myself. I smiled as I thought of myself as being too smart for prison.

"Do they still have their microchips?" I asked and Jan looked a little confused by my question. I elaborated, "The Mini Siren's will catch them if they do. That's what my group has been

121

talking about lately with the last escape attempt." Jan nodded in agreement and said, "They probably do. Not sure how they're going to get past that problem though. I guess even though it is impossible to escape this place, prisoners get desperate and try anyway."

She was right. It seemed that the prisoners were on edge all the time because of the guards, the strict rules and the schedules. It could drive the sanest person to lose their mind within a short period of time. It wasn't only the prison authorities but it was also watching your back constantly not knowing whether or not you've pissed someone off enough to kill you.

I knew all too well what that felt like and I hadn't even been in prison for a year by this point. I still wanted to know why Shelly was acting so strangely toward me. I knew that she couldn't be afraid of me because of the fight. I had definitely been on the losing end by the time the guards stopped us. Then, I wondered if Jan would know anything about Shelly's new attitude.

"Has anyone been talking about the fight I got into with Shelly?" Jan looked as if she thought I'd never ask. She eagerly responded, "Yes, people are talking about it. That's all people have been talking about over the last few days. According to what I've been hearing, Shelly's on her last strike." I was confused by this because I had no idea what a strike was. There was nothing written about it in the pamphlet of rules and regulations.

I asked, "And what does that mean exactly?" Jan looked as if she expected my question, "It basically means that if she does one more thing out of line, she ends up being moved to Cell Block D permanently." She noticed the blank look on my face and continued to explain, "There's nothing written about three strikes and you're out but it does apply to every prisoner. I heard that after the fight was broken up and the Nurse checked her out, they took her to see the Warden."

No one had ever gone to see the Warden in person as far as

122

I knew. He never interacted with the prisoners. He simply gave commands to his army of guards to enforce the laws he has made for the prisoners to follow. I had a hard time believing it at first but the more I thought about her strange behavior, the more I wondered if it could possibly be true.

Then, I realized that the other girls from her group could possibly attack me since they might not have strikes against them. I knew that they were close and would defend each other at any cost. She could give the word and they would attack me. The next time could be a lot worse and I could get seriously hurt or killed. I became afraid for my safety once again. I felt as if this would never end.

Jan continued with information she apparently had on Shelly, "She's been in a lot of fights since she came here but the one before yours was the worse. I think that was the first time she had to meet with the Warden." I asked about the last fight and Jan looked at me and replied, "She killed the last woman that she fought."

"Was her name Mary by chance?" Jan nodded and continued, "Mary was respected by everyone here. She was an older woman who had been in prison for years. We called her wise old Mary. She was minding her business but Shelly wanted to prove something I guess. Mary was attacked and died the next day from the head injuries." This story sounded all too familiar to me. It was the same story Jaye had told me a few months ago.

I began to feel angry toward Jaye for not telling me that it was Shelly that had killed Mary. Jaye knew I was being threatened and if I had known how dangerous Shelly really was, I would have been a little more careful. I wouldn't have let my guard down after being threatened for so long. By the end of our courtyard time, I was enraged toward Jaye for holding out on information.

I knew Jaye was a good person deep down and I did enjoy talking with her but she would definitely know how I felt about keeping secrets from me. I figured in two more days, I would be out of solitary confinement and had decided to confront Jaye about this. We went back to our dark cells and I fell asleep.

# Chapter 13
# Keeping Secrets

On my seventh day, I expected to be released back to Cell Block A but was surprised to awaken to the sound of my breakfast tray being pushed through the slit in the door. I waited for the guard to comment and explain why I was still in solitary but he never did.

I took my tray and began eating the cold eggs and stale toast. I knew that eventually I would be released and the days were going a little faster now that I was able to sleep more. Plus, my thoughts were keeping me entertained rather well as I thought back to the reason I was put in this prison. I regretted getting caught but didn't regret my crime.

Once I was done with my breakfast, I knew I had another hour before shower time so I laid back down to go to sleep again. Just after I had laid down, the cell door opened up and a guard was standing on the other side. "Get up. You're free to go back to your other hell hole." It was the same guard that I had spit on during my first night at Clausdrum.

I had seen him often during my time in the courtyard watching me and waiting for me to make one wrong move. He rarely ever took his eyes off of me but I never gave him a reason to bully me. I stayed on my best behavior, mostly out of fear of the other inmates. He didn't look very happy, but then again he never did. He continued to yell for me to get up and get moving. I stood up and did exactly as he said so that he still had no reason to beat me up again like he did the first night.

I was escorted back toward the other cell blocks and through the cafeteria toward the courtyard. I saw a few prisoners working in the kitchen but the other inmates were either at their jobs for the morning or outside. The cafeteria was empty other than the workers. The guard led me through the empty large room and toward the back door to the outside.

As soon as I was outside, I saw Jaye over on the bleachers with Denise, Chris and Kerry. They looked like best friends from where I was standing. Jaye was leading the conversation and the rest of them were hanging on her every word. I was enraged.

I walked over to them, looked right at Jaye and said, "Why didn't you tell me?" Jaye knew what I was talking about and had a look of guilt as she responded, "I didn't want to worry you. I thought if you knew than you'd be too scared to fight her." Kerry interrupted, "Know what? What's going on?" Jaye ignored her as she continued, "Despite how scrawny you are, you are a survivor. I thought maybe you had a chance at beating Shelly and that she would get what she deserved for once."

I couldn't believe what I was hearing. Jaye had used me to get revenge on Shelly by hoping that I would be able to hold my own in the fight and beat her. I didn't know what to say.

After a few minutes of staring back at each other, Jaye finally softened as she said, "Look, kid, I wasn't trying to set you up. I thought that if I were to tell you that Shelly killed someone, you'd be too intimidated by her and lose. If you didn't know, you may have had a chance at winning. It wasn't completely selfish. I was looking out for you."

126

That was the most interesting way I had ever heard someone lie before. I wasn't buying the excuse for a second. I looked around the courtyard and saw the other groups standing in their places. All of them had a look of deceit in their faces as if they all had their own little secret agenda to surviving in this place and they weren't even about to tell their best friend.

At that moment I knew I couldn't trust anyone. I also realized I had to be in a group in order to stay as safe as I could. Standing alone would make me vulnerable to the other inmates that may just want to prove something. I couldn't join any of the other groups so I sat down and pretended that I believed her story.

"We're glad to have you back again." Denise said in her polite voice. It made me cringe that she was so nice. She had so much to learn about survival in prison. I responded anyway, "Thanks, it's nice to be back." Jaye smiled and put her arm over my shoulder. I realized it wasn't so bad being in this group but knew that it would never be the same. Now that I knew I could be sold out by my best friend at any moment in the future I felt differently toward them.

We sat there for a little while longer as Jaye continued on with her stories and all the others listened. I was lost in my own thoughts and wasn't really listening. Jaye asked me something but I wasn't sure what she had said. I didn't make eye contact as I mumbled to myself, "I'm gonna go to the prison store."

I got up and walked over to the guard that was standing by the entrance to the building. I asked, "Can I go to the prison store to buy some items?" He nodded and waved another guard over. He said to the other guard, "Take this prisoner to the store and bring her back here when she's done." He then looked me in the eyes and said, "She has twenty minutes."

We walked back inside and down the corridor toward the Cell Block area. I wasn't sure where the prison store was and followed the guard past the cells and toward the front of the building. We turned the corner opposite of the side where I had been taken through toward the hospital.

The prison store was located directly in front of where the cell blocks were located and to the right of the front entrance. It was a small store with a window in front and a door to the left of that. We went through the doorway and inside the store where they had shelves loaded with supplies. There was a prisoner standing at the front with a scanner and another that was stocking one of the shelves. Toward the back of the store, I saw another guard sitting in a chair glaring at me as I walked in.

I began walking through the store looking at the different items and found that there was not much selection. One shelf had some books that must have been at least forty years old. None of them appealed much to me at all. I was never one for reading much since I never had the time but I thought that I could start at this point in my life since I did have a little time in the evenings. However, I wasn't ready to purchase a book.

I noticed that each shelf was labeled with the amount of credits each item cost and I figured I had enough to buy something in the store. On one of the lower shelves, they had pads of paper, pens and notebooks. I guess that would be good for writing a letter or keeping a diary. I picked up one of the pads of paper and a pen.

I hadn't written with a pen since I was learning how to use one in the second grade. The only people that used pens in 2070 were people in prison and monks. But, it was a requirement for us to learn how to write when we were children. I wasn't very good at it but I did manage to barely pass all my writing tests in school.

I wandered through the rest of the store to see what other items I may have wanted to buy. I saw that another shelf had small hand held games but the price was absolutely ridiculous. I figured no one could afford it in their first year at the prison. Below that, I saw envelopes and stamps. That was the other item I wanted. The price wasn't too bad and I picked one of each, knowing I only had one letter to write.

I took my items to the counter where the prisoner was standing and handed my things over so she could enter the prices. She did and then she scanned my arm to deduct the cost. She said, "Your total is fifty seven credits and that leaves you with thirty two more to spend." That was the first time I knew how many credits I had been earning in prison every day. Plus, I had lost a week's worth of wages when I spent time in solitary. I realized that I had just spent more than half of the credits I had earned and only had an envelope, a pad of paper, a pen and a stamp to show for it.

The guard walked me back to my prison cell where I was able to drop off my new items and then back to the courtyard. I went back over to my friends and sat down. They all stared at me for a long time after I sat back down. I suppose they were waiting for an explanation.

"What? I needed some stuff from the store." I said. They looked away but remained quiet. Jaye asked, "So, what did you buy?" It was obvious to me that I wasn't the only one who felt that no one could be trusted. I answered, "I got some supplies to write a letter. I've been thinking about writing to my Aunt. She's the one who raised me and my sister and I'm thinking maybe she wants to hear from me."

Jaye didn't seem to believe what I had said as she stared at me with a bit of suspicion. After a couple of minutes, she continued with telling stories and keeping the conversation going between everyone. I tried to act as if nothing was wrong and included myself in the conversation as much as I could. However, I was distracted by everything that had happened over the last week and had trouble pretending that everything was okay.

The prison was really beginning to wear on me at this point and I knew something had to give. I had to get past the distrust toward my friends and the fear of the guards. As we were talking, I happened to notice that the girls from Shelly's group were whispering to each other and staring at me. I nudged Jaye's arm to get her attention. She stopped talking and looked at me waiting for me to say something but I was just staring back at Shelly's group.

Jaye looked over in the direction I was looking and then said, "Oh no. we got some trouble. You done pissed off the whole group." I then explained to the rest of my group what I knew about Shelly being taken to the Warden the night of the fight and that she only had one more strike. After that, she would be sent to Cell Block D and deemed too dangerous to be with the general population.

I knew that the other girls from her group would be after me at that point and it seemed that they already were. I had to watch my back every second of the day and never let my guard down again. I had to force myself to learn to trust my friends. Otherwise I had no protection at all. The guards could only do so much and then would punish me the same as they would punish my attacker.

After lunch we went to our jobs and I was quick to find myself back into a regular monotonous routine. However, I now had a new reason to worry about my situation in prison. Kerry attempted to help me feel better about Shelly's group by saying, "I know you're scared about the girls coming after you but if you just watch your back you'll be fine. We're looking out for you too."

I smiled but didn't feel any better about the situation. The other girls were planning something and it was obvious to everyone. I had to think of a way out of this but didn't know where to start. After work, we ate dinner and went to the showers. I was especially quiet through the rest of the day as I went through the motions and racked my brain to try and come up with a way to stay alive.

Once I was back in my cell, I stared at the items I had bought and thought about writing the letter, but I just couldn't think of what to say. I thought about telling her that I stole all her credits before I left town, but then reconsidered. She didn't have to know about that.

Then, I thought about apologizing for being such a burden on her, but I couldn't force myself to do that either. As I sat there pondering what to say in the letter to my Aunt, my mind wandered back to the hunt for Wesley.

The day after I had obtained Wesley's home address, I went by his place. As I sat outside, I saw no movement in the apartment and realized that no one was home. I decided that I would go check out his home and see if I could find any other information on where he might have been for the last few days.

I walked up to the third floor where his apartment was and knocked on the door. No one answered, which was what I was expecting, so I tried to open the door. I expected the door to be locked but to my surprise, it opened right up. He had left his door unlocked and didn't seem to be home. The situation seemed suspicious to me at the time so I was careful to check the entire apartment carefully. After looking in every room and behind every corner, I confirmed that Wesley was definitely not home.

I gave a sigh of relief and then began working quickly before anyone knew I was in the apartment. I looked around and found that it was very clean and everything had a place. Wesley was an organized person, which wasn't what I had expected. I looked in his closet and saw that his clothes were gone.

The apartment must have come furnished prior to him moving in because he didn't take anything expect for his personal belongings. There was a tablet that was mounted to the desk in the back room of the apartment, which I realized was part of the furnishings. I logged in, and began searching files for information on where Wesley may have gone.

I saw statements from his bank and applications for jobs

that were never completed. I also saw the forms from the construction job I had seen him at. In addition, there were forms for jobs at salons and beauty shops. I was confused by this until I remembered that Wesley had been traveling with a girlfriend.

She must have gotten a job at one of those places while he worked in construction. I wondered who she was but quickly refocused my energy on finding Wesley. It didn't matter who he was dating. It only mattered that I got to him and killed him as soon as possible.

I finally got into his email account by getting by his password and found that my assumption was correct on Wesley being tipped off by his friend in San Francisco. There was an email sent to Wesley from his friend. I couldn't resist and had to open it.

*Wesley,*

*It's been a long time since we've spoken. Hope everything is going good in the sunshine state. Work is good here. I just got a pay raise.*

*I'm writing to you because I met a woman who was looking for you. I told her you were in Florida and afterward I regretted it. She seemed a little suspicious and said she went to school with us. I don't remember her but she's coming after you about something. Not sure what.*

*Take care and be careful,*
*George*

I was a little offended by the description of me as being suspicious but quickly got over it and refocused my search for where Wesley could be. I continued to search for any evidence of where he may have ran off to. I found another email Wesley had sent to someone titled 'Relocating Again.' It was addressed to someone named Charles. I opened it.

132

*Charles,*

*I'm still being followed by Kate's sister. I think she's really insane and could be dangerous. She just won't give up. I was at work and she saw me so I haven't been able to return to my job. Sarah and I are leaving tonight to head up to Maryland and I was hoping we could stay with you until we can get a place of our own. We'll be there at noon tomorrow.*

*Take care,*
*Wesley*

I was really offended by Wesley's description of me but my shock at the fact that he knew I had been following him was far greater. I couldn't believe that he knew I had been tracking him, however, this explained why he had moved so often. Every time I was close on his trail and ended up in the city he was living in, he moved to another city.

I sat down to take in this information I had on his whereabouts and how he knew I was after him. As I thought about it, my heart sunk at the thought that I'd have to go to Maryland to find him. My father was in Maryland and had been since before I was born. I had never been there myself and I never wanted to meet my father, but knowing that I would be in the same state as him made me think about a little more. I would be so close to where my father was being held on a life sentence and I had the opportunity to see him face to face.

I was angry at my father for abandoning me and not being there when I was growing up. I knew that he hadn't made the choice to spend his life in prison but he did make the choice to commit the crime that put him there. For the first time in my life, I wanted to tell him how I felt.

I forced myself to focus on my mission and not think about my father. He wasn't the one I was after. I had to catch up with Wesley. I sat there for a little longer while I thought about how I

133

would get to Maryland. I had been working in Florida for about a year and making decent pay. I had been stealing food and clothes as I always did, mostly out of habit, so I had saved most of my credits.

I went back over to the computer and logged into my bank account. I was pleasantly surprised to see that I had more than enough in my account to get to Maryland and even a little extra to get settled in somewhere. I made the plan to leave that night and before the sun set I was on my way to Maryland to meet up with Wesley.

As the train took off, I became anxious at the thought that I was this close. I wasn't sure what I was going to do once I found him. I had been so caught up in the chase that I hadn't really thought about how I would carry out the other half of my plan. As the train headed toward my destination, I contemplated on different ways that I could kill him.

I decided that before I could kill him, I'd have to stalk him. I needed to know what his daily schedule and routine was. I also had to make sure he was alone when I carried out my plan. I didn't want any witnesses, of course, so he had to be alone at the time. I figured that after watching him for a little while, I would be able to figure out the rest of the plan. As the train traveled over two hundred miles per hour toward Maryland, I fell asleep.

# Chapter 14
# Stalking My Prey

After being back in the general population for almost a week, I found that I had a new challenge to face. Shelly had been brought back out of solitary a couple of days after I had been released and she seemed to have her group watching every move I made. Whether I was in the courtyard, mealtime or going to the showers in the evening time, they were watching me.

They definitely wanted me to know they were watching because they weren't hiding the constant glares and whispering anytime I glanced over in their direction. My safety was once again at risk and I knew it. Shelly never gave me anymore threats and actually avoided coming close to me. She would glare at me and whisper to her friends but never approached me like she had before. I figured the rumors I had heard about her having one more chance before being sent to Cell Block D were true.

I tried to ignore the looks I was getting and stayed focused on my friends and my work each day. I also continued to ponder the idea of writing a letter to my Aunt. I had the supplies to write that letter but just couldn't think of what to say. I never brought it up to anyone in my group because I wasn't sure if they would even have the advice to give me in the situation. I debated in my mind everyday on whether to write a letter or not.

Sometimes I would just sit there at my table in the evenings and stare at a blank page in my pad of paper until they called for lights out. I began having nightmares about my past life prior to Clausdrum. I dreamed about my sister, my Aunt and our childhood. I would also see Wesley in my sleep from time to time. I never felt guilty or even wrong about what I had done to him and knew that I would do it again if given the chance.

I remembered the anxiety I felt as I stepped off the train in Maryland and knew I was right on his trail. This time, there was no one that could tip him off about me being in the same state as him. Therefore, I knew he wouldn't run to another location as long as I kept myself hidden well. I had planned once again to go to different construction sites and look for him.

The first thing I had to do when I arrived in Maryland was get a job. Maryland was a small but very busy state. Certain areas of the state looked as if they were behind the times by thirty years or more. There were small buildings and a few bars lining the street where I had found a place to stay and a train that ran right behind my small apartment. I was living in the county but frequently traveled to the city looking for Wesley.

The city was much larger than the one where I was originally from but smaller than San Francisco and Orlando. They had tall buildings and a World Trade Center just past the harbor area where cruise ships would dock. After a few weeks of traveling to the city each day, I saw no sign of him. I eventually moved on to another area of Maryland to search. I began looking in the county closer to where I was staying.

Each week, I'd go to a different area and search job sites with no luck of seeing Wesley. Then, one day, my luck changed. I walked along a construction site, being careful to stay hidden by the trees on the outskirts of the site, and I saw him working quite a distance away from where I was standing. I remained hidden as I studied him to be sure that it was Wesley. After a few moments, I knew it was him. I had found Wesley Strand once again. I now knew his place of employment and knew I could tract him easily as long as he didn't see me.

I was working at a small bar as a waitress in the area I was living in so I had most of the day to watch Wesley and find out where he was living. It seemed that his job was Monday through Friday during the day, which made it even easier to keep a close eye on him. My job was mostly on the weekends and only in the evenings a few times per week.

About a week after I had discovered where Wesley was working, I decided that I needed to know where he was living. I didn't want to take the chance of asking his co-workers or his boss since I now knew that he was aware of the fact that I had been tracking him. Plus, I didn't have a car and he drove to work each day. Every time I was able to arrive at the job site before seven in the morning, I would see him pull up in a white pickup truck with construction supplies in the cab.

I went to his job site at least three times in the first week in order to ensure the fact that he didn't skip town without me knowing it. After about a week of debating on how I could follow him home, I decided to have a cab drive me the first time. That way I would at least know where he lived. I never did get my driver's license because I never could afford a car. I had considered renting a car but knew they'd ask to see a license. It seemed my only option was a cab.

I observed him to find out what his normal hours of work were and found that most days he would leave between five and five thirty. I called a cab company and had them meet me at the job site. I didn't want the cab driver to know that I was stalking someone so I lied. "Can we wait for a few minutes? My friend is working and said he would meet me here for a ride. I'll pay for you to wait."

It seemed that I probably didn't have to make up a story for the driver since he seemed content as long as he was getting paid. He shrugged and put the car in park. I sat in the back seat and could see Wesley packing up his things to leave work for the day. The cab driver asked, "So, what address are you going to?" I panicked at first but came up with another lie. "This may sound a little strange but I don't know the address exactly. I know what roads to take and can direct you how to get there."

The cab driver seemed content with that as well. As soon as Wesley pulled out, I said, "Well, I guess my friend isn't coming after all. We can just go." I then directed him to turn around and take the road to the end where I saw Wesley heading. Wesley turned left and I instructed the cab driver, "Turn left up ahead." Wesley went straight though the light and I said nothing to the cab driver. We also went straight through the light.

I was nervous as I was hoping we wouldn't lose Wesley but we had every green light on the way and stayed on his trail. Once we were in a residential neighborhood with nice town homes and well cared for lawns, Wesley stopped in front of his home. I instructed the cab driver to head straight up the road and that my destination was a mile down the road on the right hand side. I slouched down a little and turned my head as we drove past Wesley.

The cab driver did just as I had instructed and pulled over to the right about one mile ahead from where Wesley had stopped. He scanned my arm and I got out of the cab. Once he drove off, I began walking back toward Wesley's home. I knew I had to stay hidden so I walked beyond some bushes behind the town homes and counted them as I walked toward Wesley's.

Once I thought I had the right one, I peered inside. This was definitely Wesley's home. I saw him inside sitting in the living room watching TV. He yelled something to someone in the other room but I couldn't hear him through the thick glass windows. I couldn't see who the other person was but figured it was his girlfriend. I still didn't know her identity.

His home was clean and everything was kept in order. He had nice furniture that probably came with the townhouse since he had only been in Maryland for about five months by this point. I figured he hadn't had the time to purchase high quality furniture like he had in this new home and he brought nothing with him but necessities and clothes. He said something again and then got up to go into the other room where he sat down at a table and began eating.

I tried to see who his girlfriend was but she was sitting in such a way that I could only see the back of her. From what I could see, she was petite with short brown hair. They seemed happy together. They ate their dinner while they talked and laughed with each other. I felt myself becoming angry. How could he end up with a happy life and be so right for someone when he was so horrible to my sister.

I left only after a short time to process the information I had obtained on him. Once I was back at my small apartment, I thought more about how I would carry out my plan. I not only needed to know his schedule but I needed to know hers as well. I did not want any witnesses and was hoping that there would be times that he would be alone.

Over the course of the next few weeks, I watched them in order to learn their daily routines. Apparently, from what I had found out, she was working in a hair salon nearby and her schedule was a little more sporadic than his. There were times that she would work on the weekends until late in the evening and other times she would work during the day. I really didn't have access to her schedules and thought it would be too much of a risk to investigate.

At times, while I sat in my apartment alone, I would think about my father. He was close by serving his sentence for murder. I never knew the details of his case before and had not had any desire to find out. However, now that I was so close to where he was, I was beginning to become more curious. After another couple of weeks of debating on when and how to kill Wesley, I decided I would look up my father's criminal record to learn more.

I logged into the tablet that was mounted onto my desk and typed in his name under the search area. His information and mug shot came right up on my computer. He was apparently convicted of the murder of a man named Robert Luguini in October 2043. I had never heard of this man and had no idea why my father had killed him. I was angered once again at the fact that my father had not been there for me when I was growing up. He chose a life of crime over me. I shut the computer down and went to bed.

I laid there for a while thinking about the man my father had killed and wondered why he had committed this crime. The more I thought about it the more I wrestled with the idea of meeting him. Then, I thought about how things would appear to the police if they found out I was in Maryland at the time Wesley was killed.

I realized that by visiting my father I could give a good reason for being in Maryland at the time and perhaps that would create a decoy of some sort. The police would not suspect me if they thought I was in Maryland to meet my father. It would just look like a coincidence to the police that we were in the same state at the time of Wesley's death.

I decided that I would go and meet my father. I didn't go right away because I was too nervous. I wasn't sure what to say or even if he would be upset about meeting me. At that point in my life I had never even seen the inside of a prison so I had no idea what to expect.

I was less nervous about killing Wesley. I still had no idea how to carry it out. I knew that getting a gun was out of the question since it would raise too many questions. I also knew that poisoning him wasn't a possibility either. I'd have to actually be inside his house and make food for him to eat. That idea was thrown out after only a few seconds. That left me with only one way to eliminate him. I would have to beat him to death.

He was much larger than me so I knew I'd have to have something to hit him with and I'd have to catch him by surprise. The only problem with having a weapon to hit someone with is concealing it. I had no car so I'd either take a cab or walk to his house on the night I would kill him. It would look suspicious if someone saw me walking down the street with an iron pipe or a hammer. I figured I'd come up with something eventually and continued to stalk him at every chance I had.

For the next couple of weeks, I prepared myself to meet my father. I had the address of the prison and looked up the visiting hours. Apparently, he was in a maximum security prison and there were limited visiting hours with strict rules.

I could only visit on the weekends so I glanced through the procedure for visiting. I found that I would be escorted by a guard to the visiting area where I would then speak to my father through a glass wall with a small speaker mounted within it. The speaker would pick up both of our voices so that we could communicate to each other.

I wasn't ready to meet him but I planned to visit on a Saturday and called a cab that morning. I had to be there by noon when visiting hours started. I only had two hours to say everything to my father that I wanted to say. I waited outside for my cab feeling very nervous about the reunion. As soon as the cab pulled up, I got inside and headed toward the prison where my father was being held.

Back in my prison, I had survived yet another week and a half and was managing to stay out of trouble. One evening, after I had finished with my shower and was heading back to my cell, I heard some yelling and shouting coming from one of the other cell blocks.

I had been walking down the corridor of Cell Block A when I heard the commotion. As I stood there wondering what was happening, the guards that had been at the end of the row began running full speed toward the sounds. Then, some of the prisoners started running over to see what was happening.

I didn't move. As I stood there trying to figure out what was happening, a prisoner came running back over to where I was standing and with much excitement and adrenaline said, "It's a mass breakout! The prisoners and guards are fighting and I think we're winning!"

She ran back toward the chaos and I couldn't resist following her. I ran just behind her and turned the corner to see prisoners and guards lashing it out with each other. I looked toward the other side of the cell blocks where I saw a few women running as fast as they could toward the front entrance to the prison.

I realized at that moment that those women had started this mass chaos in the effort to distract the guards and escape. It was working and I was impressed. I stood there keeping my distance as I watched the entire plan unfold right before my eyes.

A few minutes into the fight, the sirens sounded throughout the entire prison. The guards were definitely losing at this point since they were outnumbered by the prisoners. They were getting punched and shoved and there was blood everywhere.

The guards had a disadvantage because they couldn't use their Tazer guns on the prisoners. Each gun carried six Tazer darts and was meant for long range shooting or detaining one prisoner at a time. Plus, the prisoners were right on top of the guards so that they couldn't access the Tazer guns and aim properly.

The prisoners, however, were using homemade weapons against the guards that looked like rocks that were placed inside of a small piece of clothing. They were using it to whack the guards over the head. I saw a couple of prisoners with small knives that I assumed must have come from the kitchen.

I wanted no parts of the fight whether the prisoners were going to win or not. I was too afraid of being put back in solitary. I had been traumatized by that experience and never wanted to go through it again. As I stood there, I saw the Warden come down the hallway with about twenty more guards. He must have called them in on emergency. They headed straight toward the prisoners that were attacking. He began shouting orders immediately and sounded like a drill sergeant.

"What in the devil is going on here? We need these prisoners detained immediately. Men, start firing and don't miss!" The next thing I knew, Tazer darts began flying at high speeds toward the prisoners and guards. One prisoner went down in convulsions, then another and another. At one point, I saw one guard get hit in the back by one of the Tazer darts as he fell to the ground.

They were chipping away at the chaos and they had plenty of back up for the job. Each time a guard emptied his Tazer gun another guard had a fully loaded one to hand over. They were using extraordinary teamwork to fight back. I figured once they detained most of the prisoners, the rest would be easy for the guards to overcome.

As I watched the prisoners fall to the ground with Tazer darts sticking out of their bodies, I was glad that I had decided not to be involved in this scheme. The Warden then asked the guard standing next to him, "Did they catch the women who ran?" The guard nodded and the Warden then said, "Once you get this mess cleaned up, I want them in my office immediately." At that, the Warden turned around and walked back out toward the exit of the prison.

As the prisoners were falling and the guards were gaining the upper hand, I saw that one of the guards wasn't moving. It was a woman who I had seen before patrolling the areas during the evenings after shower time. She was laying there in a pool of blood. At first, it was impossible to tell if it was her blood or the blood of the other guards but after a few moments of studying the scene, it was obviously hers.

The other guards saw this as well and began shouting for help. "We need the Nurse over here now! Call an emergency team from the mainland!" A few of them yelled for assistance while the other guards herded prisoners back to their cells. I voluntarily went back to mine before they had the chance to think I was involved in any way. I had to remain on my best behavior.

As soon as we were in our cells, the doors shut and locked behind us and there was an announcement that we were all on strict lock down until further notice. At least I had already gotten my shower. Some of the women never had the opportunity to get called to the shower area prior to the fight breaking out. I stood there at my cell bars and looked out as the guards continued to try and recuperate from the experience.

Many of the guards were wiping blood off of their faces and uniforms and I figured there would be a few with bruises the next day. At approximately nine o'clock, the Warden came down to our section of the prison with a guard at each side. He was obviously going to make an announcement about the event. He stood at the far end and shouted. He could have used a microphone but he chose to use his lungs instead.

"Attention all you scum! I do not appreciate being made to look like a fool in my own domain! I will not tolerate this kind of behavior again. Since I don't know who is responsible for this chaotic, insane, animal like behavior that occurred here tonight, I will be punishing everyone." My heart sunk. I couldn't imagine what he could do to punish every prisoner. There weren't enough cells in solitary to confine us all.

He continued, "From now on, you will not receive any breakfast or lunch until further notice. Courtyard time will be cut down to only one hour per day and the remaining time you will either be at your jobs or in your cells. Furthermore, you will not be allowed in the prison store and those who work in the prison store will be reassigned to new jobs starting immediately. This will be your new routine until I decide to give you any privileges back again."

My stomach began growling at the thought of only receiving one meal per day and I wondered how long this would go on. He then turned and walked toward the other cell blocks and announced the same in front of their rows. I sat back down on my bed and thought about what had just occurred. I couldn't believe what I had witnesses. Several guards injured. One guard probably dead and a few prisoners fleeing.

I figured it would be a long time before we would get our meals back again. In the meantime I'd have to make due with only one meal in the evening. Our showers weren't taken away but our shopping privileges were. I looked over at the blank paper and the envelope once again and was glad that I had already bought it prior to this event. However, I still did not know what to say to my Aunt.

Throughout the rest of the evening, the guards kept a close eye on all the prisoners as they frequently walked past our cells and peered in at us. I wasn't up to anything unusual of course so they walked past mine without any trouble, but I heard them yell at a prisoner as they approached her cell. I couldn't tell what they were saying but there were a few guards that were in an uproar over something.

I figured that I would hear about it the next day in the courtyard from Jaye. Somehow she always knew exactly what was going on all the time in the prison. As I thought more about it, I realized that the fight must have been related to the plan I had been told about when I was in solitary confinement.

I had met Jan, one of the women from the gossiper's group, and she had mentioned that there were a few women who were planning another escape attempt. Obviously, they had failed with their plan just as the rest of the attempts had in the past. I listened as the commotion finally died down and soon I feel asleep.

# Chapter 15
# The Murder

The next morning felt strange since we weren't allowed to leave our cells after cleaning and getting dressed. We were instructed to stay on lock down until further notice. After about four hours of just sitting in my cell staring at the wall in front of me, the guards came around and began opening only certain cells. Mine was one of the cells that they opened.

We were instructed to file out through the cafeteria and to the courtyard. This was our one hour for the day to be outside. It was probably about half of the prisoners in the entire building that were let out at this time. The other half had been let out first thing in the morning after we had cleaned our cells. They were taken to their jobs for the morning shift.

I went outside and found Jaye and the others heading for the bleachers. I joined in and we all sat down in our usual place. Jaye started, "So, does anyone know who started that fight last night?" No one seemed to know except for me. "I might." I said as they all looked at me with new found curiosity. "So, what do you know?" Jaye asked.

"When I was in solitary, I met one of the gossipers and she had told me that there were a few women who were planning an escape. They thought it would be a good idea because no one would expect an escape attempt so soon after a failed one. She had told me that the women were planning something big. If this wasn't it, I'd hate to be around to see the real plan. I think they were the ones responsible for this and they got us all in trouble."

Everyone in my group sat quietly as they processed what I had just told them when Chris spoke up, "Those women should pay. We shouldn't be punished. They should be punished." We were a little surprised at Chris' outward expression of the situation but she was absolutely right. We shouldn't be the ones to pay for their mistakes. "I wonder if there is a way to prove that they were the ones behind all this so that we're not suffering for it." I mentioned.

Denise replied, "We should at least give it a try. There's no reason for all of this." Jaye didn't seem very convinced by our argument. "I don't know if that will help. There were a lot of prisoners that were in on the fight without even realizing that someone was trying to escape. They were rallied to do it and one guard is dead now. I think the Warden is outraged about that more than the escape."

She was right. The Warden was outraged and he seemed to be the type of person who would make everyone suffer just because he held that power. Plus, a lot of women were involved in the fight and who knows which one of them actually killed the guard. Many of the prisoners had makeshift weapons and I wondered where they had gotten them from.

"How did they get the weapons to fight the guards?" I asked. Kerry answered, "I think the women who were rallying the fight may have been the ones that gave them out. When we were leaving for the showers after dinner, I saw them handing over one of the weapons. I was able to stand nearby and could hear what was said. Apparently, it was a heavy stone placed inside of a sock."

"And that was only one weapon. I saw someone with a sharp object of some kind that sort of looked like a knife. It couldn't have been of course since they don't allow that in the prison but I think someone had made it somehow." Denise added. "It could have been from the kitchen. They have pairing knives and the prisoners who do the cooking have access to them." I said. "I learned that from the woman who is in Cell Block D. She killed her co-worker with one a few years ago when she tried to escape."

Everyone seemed very impressed with the information I had gotten and we continued to talk about it for a few more minutes before we were called to go back to our cells once again. We were to sit in our cells for another three hours before we could go to our jobs. I was beginning to appreciate the job I had, after being in solitary with nothing to do and now lock down.

Every day during lockdown was the same routine of sitting in our cells waiting for our hour of courtyard time and then waiting to go to our jobs. We were let out in the evenings to take our showers and herded back to our cells for the night. We only received one meal per day and the Warden didn't seem to care about the hunger pains we were all feeling.

There was one woman who had to be taken to the hospital because she passed out during her work. According to the gossip that was going around about it, she had low blood sugar and could have died from it. They had taken her to the hospital for the Nurse to treat her and I assume that she got an extra meal that day.

Each day I thought more about my adventures on the outside while I was chasing down Wesley. I had ended up in Maryland and spent about six months stalking him and his girlfriend, while waiting for the perfect opportunity to move in on him and finish him off. My father was being held in the Maryland State Penitentiary so I had called a cab and was heading to the prison to meet him for the first time. I was beyond nervous.

As we pulled up to the prison, I felt a sense of despair from the site of it. It was a single story building but enormous in size. There was a barbed wire fence around the perimeter that had signs saying 'high voltage'. I couldn't see the back of the building so I wasn't sure what the courtyard looked like but there were armed guards everywhere. We drove up to the entrance where a guard asked who we were visiting before opening the gate for us. I told him and he opened the gate. The cab driver pulled up to the front entrance to the building and stopped to let me out.

As I walked up to the front entrance, the guards asked who I was visiting once again and I told them. They let me in and another guard escorted me to the visitor's area. It was a small room where they searched the visitors before letting them into yet another room with small cubicles and glass separating the visitors from the prisoners. I was searched and then instructed to go through the door to the actual visiting room. A guard walked me past three cubicles before having me sit at the fourth one from the entrance. The seat on the other side was empty and the guard said, "Wait here."

I sat there for about ten minutes before I saw the door on the other side open and a middle aged man walk up to the cubicle I was sitting at. He sat down in the chair across from me and stared at me through the glass. He was a tough looking man that had probably lived a rough life by the looks of it. He had gray hair combed back and a gray beard. He looked as if he hadn't slept in weeks. I felt extremely awkward as I stared back. I didn't know how to start the conversation. Finally, I forced myself to say, "Carol Wheeler?" He nodded. This was my father.

My heart was racing as I struggled with what to say. I continued to speak. "I'm Roxanne Beatry." I waited for him to have some recognition of the name but he just stared back at me. I continued, "I'm your daughter." "I don't have a daughter." he said with little emotion to his words. He acted as if I had made a casual mistake.

"Yes, I am. My mother is Barbara Beatry. Don't you remember her?" He suddenly had a look of recognition as he responded, "Oh, yeah. I do remember Barbie. Wow, I hadn't heard

150

from her since I was put in this place." He looked at me and smiled. "So, you really are my daughter?"

"Yes. She never told you about me?" "Nope. I never got a phone call, visit or even a letter. She never bothered to tell me." He still seemed slightly absent as he spoke. It was almost as if he had been in prison for so long that he had lost his own characteristics that were replaced with complacency. "Well, she ran out on me too. She had another kid and we were both raised by our Aunt. I haven't seen or heard from her in years." He didn't seem to care much about my childhood. He just stared back at me and said nothing.

I figured I'd change the subject. Maybe he'd be more interested in talking about himself. "How did you end up in prison?" He looked back at me and, with no expression on his face, he simply said, "I killed a man. Shot 'em dead. He was taking too long at the toll booth and I wasn't happy about it. I got out of my car with my gun, walked up to his window and pulled the trigger."

"You didn't even know him?" I asked in disbelief at my father's honesty. "Nope. Never seen him before in all my life. Cops took me in right there on the spot. I guess I was just stressed out and snapped." I couldn't believe what he had just admitted to me. He acted as if it wasn't even wrong. He spoke about it as if it were just a common occurrence that could have happened to anyone.

"Do you ever regret what you did?" I asked out of curiosity. I must have struck a nerve with him by my question. He immediately became emotional and angry as he responded, "What are you here for? You got a hundred questions to ask me? What's wrong with people like you coming in here from your free world and harassing me?" He continued yelling as two guards came running into the room to detain him before his anger escalated any further.

As they pulled him back from the glass, he got his arm free and started beating the glass as if he were trying to break through it. I jumped up and stepped back. I watched in horror as my father

151

tried to attack. Another guard from my side of the glass came over to escort me back out of the room.

He didn't say a word as we hurried back to the room where I had been searched. Once we were away from my father, I asked, "Can you tell me what I said that made him go off like that?" The guard replied, "There's no predicting Carol. No one knows when he'll have an outburst like that. Don't take it personally."

Somehow I couldn't apply the advice the guard had given me. Once I had gotten back to my apartment, I laid there wondering what was wrong with my father. I replayed the conversation over and over but couldn't seem to understand what had set him off. I was starting to regret the visit I had with him but realized that I would have regretted it more if I hadn't have gone to see him. After thinking about the events over in my mind, I eventually fell asleep.

After I had met my father and stalked Wesley for a little more than six months. I finally felt ready to carry out the rest of my plan. I had thought about it enough and knew my plan would work. His girlfriend sometimes worked late into the evening and I picked a night that she wouldn't be at home. I stood outside of his home and peered in through the back door while I waited for him to go upstairs to bed.

After watching him for quite some time, I learned that he always went to bed early whether his girlfriend was home or not. From where I was standing, I couldn't see into the room he was in. I could only see the reflection of the television. It was the best place to stand without anyone seeing me. I figured I'd wait until the television went off. Then, I'd wait a few more minutes before making my move.

I had no weapon with me to use because I knew that I would bring attention to myself by carrying one to his house. I decided that I would find something in his home to beat him with. All I needed was one strong whack over the head to knock him out.

Then, I could continue to hit him until I knew I had finished him off.

I had thought about this plan over and over in my head and couldn't find any flaws. He would probably go upstairs to bed at about nine o'clock and his girlfriend wouldn't be home until after ten. She would come home and find him dead.

As I stood there patiently, the television turned off. I barely saw his shadow as he went from the den to the stairs to go to bed. My heart began to race. I waited approximately ten minutes and then I went around to the side of the house where I found a small window with no lock.

It was too small for most people to get through but I was smaller than most people. I fit through with only a slight amount of squeezing. There was nothing to stand on once I was through the window and I fell to the floor.

I froze as I wondered if Wesley had heard me coming into the house. As I sat there, I heard shuffling coming from upstairs. He had heard me and was coming to find out what had caused the noise. I had to hide. I was in the kitchen and saw the food pantry to my left. I squeezed my body into it and closed the door. I could see through the pleated slits in the pantry door and saw him sneaking down the stairs with a baseball bat in his hands.

I watched him walk through the house looking from side to side with the baseball bat ready to hit the first person he saw. He walked through the living room, turned on the light and checked behind the doors. He walked through the kitchen looking under the table.

He went back into the den where I couldn't see him and then came back around to the stairs. He stood there for another minute before he relaxed his shoulders, turned off the lights and leaned the bat against the banister. Then, he headed back up the stairs.

This was my chance and I had to take it. I quietly walked around to the stairs and picked up the bat, careful to not make a sound. I followed him up the stairs in the dark as quietly as I could. Being that close to Wesley caused my heart to race faster than it ever had before. As we reached the top of the stairs, I noticed that the bedroom light was still on.

I was directly behind him and he didn't know it, until he saw my shadow. He turned toward me as I swung the bat as hard as I could against the temple of his head. His legs gave out on him and he collapsed to the floor. I continued to beat him over and over again. Blood was everywhere as his skull crushed in and his face became unrecognizable.

I couldn't stop hitting him. All the anger I felt over the last four years had suddenly surfaced and no one could stop me at this point. My mind was not mine anymore as I pounded his head repeatedly as hard as I could. Then, I felt the weakness come over my own body and my legs gave out beneath me.

I fell to my knees next to his body and cried. I was covered in blood and he laid there lifeless. I had done what I came here to do and now I had no purpose. After spending four years tracking him, then stalking him, I felt empty when I knew it was over.

I refocused after a few minutes, realizing that his girlfriend would be there at any moment. I had to clean myself up and leave. I went into the bathroom and began washing the blood off of my face when I noticed that my shirt was also covered in blood.

I decided that I would take one of his girlfriend's jackets, wear that over my shirt until I got home and then throw away the clothes I was wearing. After I had washed up, I left the baseball bat by his body and went downstairs to look for a jacket. I found one in the hall closet and left his house by nine forty five.

Once I was back at my apartment, I sat there wondering what I would do with the rest of my life. I replayed the events and was sure that I had left no evidence. I had been wearing gloves so my fingerprints wouldn't be found on anything in his house. No one else was home so I was sure there were no witnesses. I felt as though I was safe from being accused of this crime.

However, I couldn't shake the emptiness I felt. I had spent such an enormous amount of my time chasing after this one person that I thought about nothing else. I hadn't realized how much emotion I had invested in the hunt for Wesley Strand. Now that it was over, there was nothing left for me to obsess over.

I fell asleep thinking about what I would do for the rest of my life. When I woke up the next morning, I decided that I would head back to my hometown. I had friends there that I hadn't seen in four years. I checked my bank account and airline costs and found I had more than enough to get back home. I purchase my ticket and left that same day.

As the airplane took off, the emptiness I had felt at first was beginning to subside. A feeling of excitement was replacing it as I thought about my hometown. I couldn't wait to see my old friends and my old neighborhood. They would probably have questions about where I had gone and I decided that I would just tell them that I wanted to see other places before settling down.

I'd tell them about the cities I had been to and the people I had met over the last four years. I thought perhaps I could come up with stories to tell them about my experiences in the other cities. They would believe me and I was confident that no one would ever suspect that I had anything to do with the murder of Wesley Strand.

# Chapter 16
# The Only Escape

Over the next several days on lock down, we were becoming more agitated as the hunger pangs and boredom were getting to us. I didn't know how much more of this torture I could take. Each day went by more slowly than the one before it. Being on lock down was still better than my week in solitary, but it had been more than a week on lock down and the Warden hadn't called it off yet. I felt as if he never would.

Once I was at my job, Kerry and I spoke for a while about the incident and tried to come up with a rational reason why the prisoners thought they could get away once again. I just couldn't imagine what would possibly make someone believe that they could escape the Mini Sirens and the guards.

It had been attempted a few times since Clausdrum had reopened and no one yet had been successful at getting to the mainland. If the Mini Sirens didn't catch a prisoner escaping, then that prisoner would have to survive the currents of the ocean and the freezing cold waters.

If they managed to escape to the other side and survive the elements, there would definitely be Police just on the other side tracking their microchips. It seemed to me that escaping

Clausdrum was an impossible task. I shuttered at the thought of what would happen to the women who tried.

In solitary, the four women who had failed an attempt prior to this last one had been in solitary for weeks and had still not been released after I was taken back to the general population. I had only been there for one week and was already going insane from the isolation and darkness. I couldn't even fathom what it would be like to spend several weeks in that hole.

Both Kerry and I agreed that the punishment for attempting to escape was far greater than the small possibility of gaining freedom. Even though I was miserable and beginning to lose my mind with each day I spent in prison, I couldn't imagine trying to run. The guards would tract anyone who tried.

Kerry had explained that there was a computer room that contained several computers with everyone's microchip number entered into it. There were guards that sat in the room and watched the screens to make sure every prisoner was exactly where they should be at all times. I wasn't sure where Kerry had learned this information and I didn't ask.

After our work was completed for the day, we were taken back to the cafeteria for dinner and then showers. In the shower area, I tried to move quickly through in order to avoid Shelly at all costs. I wasn't sure if she was crazy enough to take the chance at attacking again but I wasn't about to find out. I hadn't let my guard down since I was brought back to the general population.

Once we were back in our cells for the night, I laid there and thought about writing the letter to my Aunt but fell asleep before I decided on what I would even say. I slept well that night and dreamed about being free. I saw myself running toward the ocean, swimming across and escaping to the mainland. In my dream, there were no guards or police chasing after me. It was the most pleasant dream I had had since my first day at Clausdrum.

I woke up the next morning and began cleaning my cell right away as the guards watched us and counted each prisoner. I had forgotten at first that we were not going to be let out immediately for breakfast and my stomach began growling at the thought of going all day with no food. This was the second week of lock down and I was already wondering whether or not I would make it for much longer.

The day went by slowly as I sat in my cell most of the time and then went to work. During our work, we didn't talk much about anything specific. We just worked diligently and tried to handle our own hunger the best way we could. Dinner would be served after our work was done.

As we started walking back up the stairs to the cafeteria once again, we all froze as we heard the horrible sounds of screaming. It didn't sound like a normal scream of pain or fear. It was a scream of extreme terror and agony. I had never heard a sound such as this one before in my life. I had chills as he hair on my body stood up at the horrific sound.

Officer Yander instructed us to keep moving even though we were frozen in place and afraid to go any further. We forced our legs to keep moving up the stairway toward the sounds of screaming that seemed to pierce our ears. As we moved up the stairs to the entrance of the cafeteria, the screaming seemed to be coming closer.

Just as we reached the very top and came through the doorway, I saw where the screaming had been coming from. It was one of the women who had been in solitary for the attempted escape. She had been in solitary for a few weeks by this point and had probably been slowly losing her mind.

I froze at the site as I saw two guards leading her down the hall, past the cafeteria and toward the front entrance. I assumed by the site of it that they were taking her to the hospital. She was covered in blood and screaming like a mad woman. It didn't seem

158

to be the screams of pain but it was the screams of a woman who had lost her mind.

As I looked closer at the site when she walked past me, I saw that her left arm had been completely filleted. I could see the skin of her forearm was torn unevenly from her wrist to her elbow. Beneath the open skin, I could see the muscles, fatty tissue and veins and arteries. Blood was pulsating from the wound and had covered the front of her yellow jumpsuit.

The officers rushed past us not even aware of the fact that we were standing there observing the scene. They had looks of panic on their faces as they led her away as quickly as they could. One of the officers looked as if he could pass out from the horrific site at any moment. The color was gone from his face and he appeared to be nauseous.

Once they had passed by us, I noticed that there was a small blood trail leading in the direction they had gone. "I don't think she has a chance to make it through that." Kerry said as she stood right next to me. I hadn't even realized she was there. "I know her from solitary." That was all I could think about. I had spent time in the courtyard during my punishment in solitary and saw her every day. She had an absent look and didn't speak to anyone. I wondered then if she was in the process of losing her mind.

As we remained standing at the entrance to the cafeteria trying desperately to absorb what we had just seen, a guard came walking over to us and herded us back toward the line for food. "Move it. Get in line. Show's over." She said as she pushed us away from the spot we were frozen in. We did as she instructed and got in line for our dinner.

After seeing that horrible site and all that blood, I wasn't sure if I would be able to eat my one meal for the day. My stomach was starving but my mind was disgusted. I was served meatloaf with red sauce, which didn't help to convince my mind to eat. As I stared at my meatloaf and red sauce, I pictured blood and flesh.

159

We sat down at our normal seat and put our arms to our sides and waited for the whistle to blow. As we all sat there looking at our food in disgust, I realized Jaye wasn't at the table with us. I whispered across the table to Kerry, "Where's Jaye?" She shrugged and said, "How should I know? I've been with you the whole time." She was right and I realized how ridiculous it was for me to ask her.

We managed to eat our dinner in silence as we force down the red sauce and tried desperately not to think of the blood. Afterward, we were called to the showers and sent back to our cells for yet another night. I wondered to myself how long the lock down would last but figured it couldn't be much longer. It would be inhumane to keep us from eating our three meals for an extended amount of time.

The next morning, we awoke to the sound of the whistle and began cleaning our cells. I was finished cleaning mine in less than five minutes. Since I really had no belongings and not much furniture, there wasn't much to clean. I was always finished rather quickly at my first chore of the day. I sat back down knowing that I wasn't going to be let out for another four hours.

Once it was time to go to the courtyard, I was relieved that I would get a change of scenery, even if it was only for one hour. We went outside and I met up with my group at the bleachers. Jaye wasn't outside by this time and I began to worry about her, since she hadn't been at dinner the night before either. As I sat down wondering what had happened to her, I saw her walking over toward us. I was glad to see that she was okay and realized at that moment that she was my best friend in prison.

As soon as she sat down, we bombarded her with questions on where she had been during dinner the night before. "What happened to you yesterday?" Denise asked. "I was held back at my job for a little longer." Jaye responded. I realized she had been

160

working at the hospital when the woman was brought in just as dinner was being served.

"There was an emergency and the Nurse demanded that I stay to help." At this point, Jaye had no idea that we had witnessed the woman being taken to the hospital just before we were given food. "We saw her. It was horrible. They took her past us when we were going to the cafeteria." I explained. Jaye didn't look back at me but just stared straight ahead as she thought about the woman.

"I was just about to leave to get dinner when the Nurse said I had to stay. She had gotten a radio call about the incident and had to prepare a room for her immediately. She also called the paramedics from the mainland once she realized how bad the situation was. She told me that she needed a second pair of hands to try and contain the bleeding."

We all listened intently as Jaye explained what had happened. "Apparently, the woman was in solitary and she was found by one of the guards. She had torn her own skin open with her bare hands. We're not even sure why she did it. Obviously, she wasn't looking for her microchip since everyone knows it's in the upper arm. I think she was trying to kill herself."

I couldn't imagine attempting suicide in such a horrible way as she had done but it did make sense. If she was in solitary confinement, she had no access to any type of sharp objects or supplies. She couldn't hang herself since there was nothing to tie the bed sheets to. The ceilings in solitary were smooth with no objects attached. The only option she had left was to tear her own artery open with her bare hands. She had reached in and ripped it in half.

"As soon as she arrived to the hospital, the Nurse had her chained to the chair we had prepared and instructed me to hold her arm down as tightly as I could. The woman was strong and she fought me with everything she had. As she continued to scream, the Nurse tried closing the wound and stitching it up the best she could. I couldn't even tell where the bleeding was coming from because there was so much of it."

Jaye seemed to be disturbed by what she had experienced in the hospital the night before as she spoke to us about it. I had never seen Jaye bothered by anything. Normally, she was so laid back and calm with every situation that came her way. I knew this was something even she couldn't handle. "Is she okay now?" I asked

"She didn't make it. I was holding her arm and the Nurse was stitching the wound underneath her torn muscles. The bleeding started to slow down and I thought the Nurse was fixing it. But then, I looked at the woman's face as her screaming started to get quieter and she was just staring up toward the ceiling as the life went out of her. She died right there in front of me before the paramedics could even get to the island."

Jaye had killed a person and had watched him die. She had no regrets about her actions and showed no sign of being bothered by it. She was like me in that way and I was a little confused as to why she seemed to be bothered by the death of this one inmate so much. She seemed to be traumatized by the death of this woman she didn't even know.

Jaye then looked at me and said, "Roxy, she was one of us. This place had driven her insane. It's not right." I could see the tears forming in her eyes as she seemed so distraught by the death of an inmate. I then understood how she felt. The prison itself with the rules and the punishments had driven this woman to take her own life. I secretly hoped that this situation would change things, even though I knew deep down that things would never get better for any of us.

"Did you get to eat dinner?" Denise asked. "They let me have dinner afterward but I wasn't very hungry. They brought me to the cafeteria after everyone had already finished their meals." I understood why Jaye couldn't eat much. I had trouble eating as well after I had only seen the woman for a few seconds as she passed by me.

"Something has to change around here. The way we are treated just can't possibly be legal." Kerry commented as she tried to console Jaye for having to see the prisoner die in such a horrific way. No one responded as we all sat there in silence knowing that nothing would ever change.

We were the prisoners and we had no rights. No one would ever fight for us. We didn't even have access to the outside world so we couldn't even tell anyone what was happening. Even during visiting hours, the guards watched the prisoners so closely that the prisoners couldn't say anything about the treatment to their families.

No one would ever know how horrible it was in Clausdrum. I figured I would die in this place along with everyone else but just had no idea how long I would have to wait for that day. Even though it was the only obvious escape plan that would actually work, I just couldn't imagine killing myself.

# Chapter 17
# The Visitor

After two weeks of being punished for the chaos that was caused by the prisoners and the death of one of the guards, the Warden came to the cell block to make the announcement that things were going back to normal again. We would receive our three meals each day and have the normal allotted time in the courtyard. I was relieved and actually felt rather spoiled by these privileges that I had taken for granted before. The guards were more alert than they had ever been, even when things did go back to normal, but that was expected.

However, as hard as I tried to remain invisible to them, there was one guard that began making threats. She was a large middle aged women named Officer Wiley and had a reputation for being tougher than any of the men working at Clausdrum. In fact, she had been in charge of training the new guards at one time.

After the incident involving the death of a guard, the Warden put Officer Wiley back on duty to watch over the prisoners. She would come around during the first count of the day and as she walked by my cell, she would raise her nightstick, look right at me and yell to all the prisoners "I'm watching every move you make in this place and don't think I won't use force if I have to!"

Even though she had said this to all the prisoners, I could tell by the way she glared in my direction that she was speaking specifically to me. In the cafeteria, I would see her looking over at our group as if we were causing trouble of some kind and I tried to ignore it. Eventually, I pointed it out to the others and they confirmed that I wasn't imagining it. This guard seemed as if she was out to get me. Maybe she thought I was one of the prisoners responsible for the fight that had broken out that led to the death of one guard.

I was a little worried about the guard watching me more closely but I continued to follow the rules the best I could and really didn't seek out any trouble. I was also trying my hardest to stay away from Shelly and her group. I knew that Shelly wasn't going to attack me in any way since she was on her last strike and obviously didn't want to end up in Cell Block D, but her friends were all watching me closely. I figured that her friends probably didn't have as many strikes as she did so I ran the risk of being attacked by any one of them at any moment. I was just secretly hoping that they weren't as loyal to Shelly as they seemed to be.

Another issue I had on my mind was that I still hadn't written the letter to my Aunt. I really was beginning to doubt that I ever would. The paper, pen, envelope and stamp still sat on my desk untouched. I continued to periodically contemplate on what to say to my Aunt in the letter. Then, the thought would cross my mind that she probably wouldn't read it anyway. I would then dismiss the idea of writing the letter at all.

The first day that we were back to our normal routing, I requested to go to the prison store once again. I was told I had to wait because there were two prisoners that had already gone and only two at a time were allowed. I sat back on the bleachers and waited my turn while the five of us talked just to pass the time.

"I'm so glad the lock down time is over. What do you think they'll do to the prisoners that tried to escape?" Kerry asked. "Not sure. Could be any number of punishments waiting for them." Jaye said. "Maybe they'll go to Cell Block D." Denise added.

I knew that probably wouldn't be the case from my experience in solitary, so I replied, "I don't think that will happen. Cell Block D only has two open cells and there were at least five women who planned the breakout and tried to run." I remembered back to the fight when I had seen five women running for the front entrance.

"What I don't understand is that they know they have microchips and will be tracked. Don't they realize that?" Denise asked. "You're too new here to understand." Jaye commented. "When you're here for too long, you start to lose your mind and the only thing you think about is your freedom. The guards, the routine, the work they give you can make you crazy." "And then add to it the other prisoners that seem to have it out for you." I said as I nodded over toward Shelly's group. They were all staring back at me and whispering to each other.

Everyone else looked over toward that direction and agreed when they saw how I was being singled out by the glares. A few minutes later, I was called over by the guard at the entrance to the building. It was my turn to go to the prison store. I wanted to buy some reading material.

The first time I had gone, I noticed they had old books. I had never actually seen a paper copy of a book in my lifetime, until I had gone to the prison store the first time, but there were libraries that contained them. People who had an interest in antiques and old items would often times go to libraries where you could read these types of books. I never had any interest in that.

However, in prison we had no choice since we didn't have access to computers like the rest of the world did. People on the outside read digital books on their computers or phones and rarely owned paper copies.

166

As soon as I was at the prison store, I went straight to the isle that had the paper books lined up on a shelf. There wasn't much of a selection to choose from and I was never one for reading much anyway. I just picked the book that was in the best shape since most of them were falling apart.

By the time I dropped off my book in my cell, it was time for lunch again, then work. It actually felt nice to be back to eating three meals per day. However, I wasn't able to finish my breakfast or lunch. After two weeks of only getting a small dinner each day I must have shrunk my stomach.

I noticed everyone else was leaving food behind as well. We went to our jobs just after lunch and nothing had changed with that. The hours had remained the same while we were on lock down since taking away our work each day wasn't considered a punishment.

Kerry and I spoke quietly about the problem I was having with Shelly's group staring at me and whispering to each other while we folded the clothes. I just had a gut feeling that something could happen at any time. I would get a feeling of dread every time I thought about it because I knew that if they all jumped me, they'd kill me. They probably felt safe doing so since Shelly had more than likely reassured them that they wouldn't be sent to Cell Block D. I felt as if my days were numbered.

After work, we ate dinner and then waited to be called for our showers. After I had finished my shower and had gotten dressed again, I was picking up my shoes when I felt someone bump into me from behind. I heard the person say loudly, "Excuse me!" I turned and saw it was one of Shelly's friends.

She had purposely bumped into me as she walked by. Then, another one of Shelly's friends came right behind her and did the same thing. Then, another one came after her and shoved me. They continued to shove me one after the after. I was losing my balance

167

with every shove and fell to the floor as the last one knocked into me.

I was picking myself up off the floor when I felt nails digging into my arm. Someone had a hold of me and was pulling me up with force. I heard the person yelling in my ear, "Were not going to have a problem are we, Number CL15595?" I became defensive thinking I was being attacked by another one of Shelly's friends and raised my other hand to strike back. Just before I did, I turned to see Officer Wiley two inches from my face. I put my arm down as quickly as I could and replied, "No, ma'am."

"Good, because you know what I do to fighters? Huh!?" I shook my head unable to hide the fear, "I'll kick your ass so hard you won't be able to walk for weeks!" Officer Wiley had earned her reputation for a reason and I was scared. Her reaction to the situation also confirmed to me that she did not have my safety in mind at all.

By the time I had gotten back to my cell, I was outraged. I couldn't show it, of course, but I wanted to. How could she yell at me when I didn't even cause any trouble? Didn't she realize that it was Shelly's group that was harassing me? Officer Wiley never said a word to them. She had it out for me and I didn't know why.

I was too angry that night to start reading my book and definitely did not feel like writing a letter to my Aunt. So, I went to sleep early. The next day was Saturday and we only worked for a couple of hours on Saturdays and had off on Sunday's. Visiting hours were held during the weekends and the schedule allowed time for prisoners to have visits without interrupting work hours. I never had anyone come to see me, of course, but other prisoners did from time to time. After lunch on the weekends, we were taken back to our cells for about two hours while visitors came.

The visiting area was located at the front of the prison building and a guard would escort the prisoner to that area. They had two hours to spend visiting and I had been told that there was a glass wall between them. I figured it must have been similar to the prison I had been to when I went to see my father. While prisoners were taken one by one to the visiting area, I would just take a nap in my cell. I wasn't expecting anyone so I used that time to get some extra rest and enjoy my time away from being harassed by other prisoners and the guards.

However, this particular Saturday changed my normal routine. I had been back in my cell after lunch and laid down to take a nap. Just as I was drifting off to sleep, a guard woke me saying, "Get up. You have a visitor." I couldn't believe it and thought that he had the wrong person. "No one comes to visit me." I argued. "Well, someone did today." I looked at him and said, "I'm prisoner CL15595. Are you sure?" He checked his tablet, looked back at me and replied, "I'm sure. Now get up."

I did as he instructed and walked with him to the visitor's station. I couldn't imagine who it could be. Even if my Aunt wanted to visit me, she wouldn't have enough money to purchase the plane ticket to the mainland and then the ticket for the ferry across to the island. None of my cousins would visit me either. I couldn't figure out who it could be. I was sure there had been a mistake and thought that maybe they'd realize it once I was in the visiting station.

I was escorted through the door and down a small isle to a cubicle and that's when I realized it hadn't been a mistake. It was Sarah Branson; the woman who was responsible for my conviction. I stood there frozen as I stared back at this woman and wondered what she could possibly want from me. The officer instructed me to have a seat and acted as if I had no choice. I sat down across from her and just stared at her for a few moments before I finally said, "What do you want?"

She leaned in and responded, "I just want the satisfaction of seeing that you're going to rot in hell." Well, that was constructive, I thought to myself. She came all the way out to the island to see

169

me in prison. I commented, "I guess you didn't believe the jury when they said the word guilty?!" That pissed her off.

"Guilty? Like that's enough? You took away my fiancé! You killed him in cold blood. Besides, my psychiatrist told me I should come and see you here in person. I needed the closure for myself. I just want to make sure that you will never get out of here. So help me God, if you ever get out of this place, I will come find you and kill you myself."

"That's reassuring" I mumbled half to myself with a bit of sarcasm. I was getting irritated with this conversation rather quickly. Then, I felt disbelief at the fact that Sarah had come all this way to see me. "So, you came all the way here to see that I was in a prison?" I just couldn't grasp the idea that she went out of her way to see me behind bars.

I continued "Well, I'm here. Are you happy now? Does that give you closure enough?" I said in a mocking tone. "Yes, it does." She continued to tell me how much she hated me and that she wanted me to go to hell after my life sentence was served in prison. I began to zone out and didn't hear much of anything she said. All I could think about was her hair.

It seemed strange even to me at the time, but I tuned her out and just focused on how nice her hair looked. She was about my size and very thin and I noticed that she had the same bone structure as me. Her hair was brown like mine, but she had it cut shorter. It flowed nicely down to the length of her chin but mine was almost to my waist. I hadn't heard a thing she said by the time she finished with, "…so the worms can chew on your remains!"

"Sounds lovely." I replied with sarcasm as I turned to one of the guards and nodded to let him know I was done with visiting time. I just wanted to go back to my cell and be alone until I had to go to my job. Once I was in my cell, I kept thinking about how nice her hair looked and how our faces were so similar. I decided that I would request a visit to the chop shop and see if they could cut my hair the same as hers. I knew it would look good on me. Then, I wondered if I was beginning to lose my mind in this place just as the other prisoners had.

Sarah Branson went to high school with me but she lived in the same neighborhood as Wesley. She came from a wealthy family and never wanted for anything. I had heard rumors before that she was never close to her family after high school. They were very strict and she wanted freedom so she hadn't spoken to them in years. Then, she had run off with Wesley. She was a spoiled brat in high school and always got her way no matter what. I used to be jealous of her at times.

After I had killed Wesley, went back to my hometown and was captured by the police for his murder, I was held in a jail and had court every day. They had appointed a public defender for me who didn't seem to care about my case either way. I figured my only option was to convince everyone that I had only gone to Maryland to visit my father.

No one wanted to listen to me during the trial and nothing about the case was communicated to me. I felt as though no one cared about my fate during the trial. Near the end of the case, after evidence was submitted and arguments were made against me, the prosecutor stood up and said, "Your Honor, I'd like to call the eye witness to the stand."

My world stopped in that moment as I racked my brain to figure out what witness she could possibly be talking about. Wesley had been home by himself. I walked through the house and went into his bedroom. I knew that any eye witness would have to be lying about what they saw.

The doors at the back of the court room opened and Sarah Branson walked through. She went past me without making eye contact and took a seat on the stand. After she was sworn in, the prosecutor asked, "Ms. Branson, where were you on the night that

171

Wesley Strand was killed?" She leaned forward to speak into the microphone, "I was at home with Wesley."

"Can you tell me, in your own words what happened that night?" She seemed uncomfortable by the question and still refused to make eye contact with me as she said, "Wesley and I were watching TV until about nine o'clock when we went to bed. As soon as we were settled in for the night, we both heard noises coming from downstairs." She paused for a moment before she continued.

"Wesley told me to stay in the bedroom and he would go and check it out. He was gone for quite a long time and I was scared so I got up and went into the closet to hide. After a few moments, I saw Wesley come back into the room. I was just about to come out of the closet when I saw someone behind him with a baseball bat."

The prosecutor asked, "Was it this baseball bat?" as she pointed to the evidence lined up at the front of the court room. Sarah nodded and said, "Yes, that's the one." My lawyer stood up and interrupted, "Objection, your honor. How could she possibly know that's the same bat?" "Objection sustained." The judge said. Then the judge looked at the prosecutor, "Care to reword your question?" "Sorry, your honor." The prosecutor said before addressing the witness again. "Was it a bat like this one?"

"Yes, it looked just like that one. The person hit Wesley and continued to hit him until he wasn't moving. Then, she went into the bathroom where I think she was getting cleaned up, since I heard running water. Afterward, she left the house and that's when I called 911" She took a deep breath as she seemed to have accomplished the most uncomfortable task of her life.

The prosecutor continued, "Can you tell me, Ms. Branson, is the person who killed Wesley Strand in this court room today?" She nodded and the prosecutor continued, "Can you point the person out to us and to the jury?" Sarah made eye contact with me for the first time as she pointed directly at me.

"Your honor, that's all the questions I have." and she sat back down. The judge asked, "Does the defendant want to cross examine the witness?" My lawyer stood up halfway as he said, "No, your honor." I was mortified. The jury went out of the court room to make their decision and seal my fate.

I knew I was going to lose at that moment and I felt as if I could pass out at any time while I waited anxiously to hear the words that would dictate the rest of my life. I wasn't surprised when they came back out and gave the verdict of 'guilty'.

# Chapter 18
# My New Look

The day after Sarah had paid me a visit, I decided I wanted to get my hair cut. The chop shop was available to prisoners every day during the week and on weekends during the visiting hours. I knew I wasn't going to have another visitor so I figured this would be a good time for me to get a haircut.

I called to a guard and expressed my request. He opened my cell and escorted me to the chop shop. I had never been there but I had seen some of the horrible haircuts other prisoners had gotten. I really didn't care if my hair cut was perfect since I didn't have a mirror anyway. I was just ready for a change.

The chop shop was located just before the cafeteria, to the left side, opposite of the stairs to the laundry area. It was a small room with barber chairs and a woman who looked as if she belonged in prison right alongside of us. She had tattoos down both of her arms, short black hair and piercings in her nose and eyebrows. She had a boxy face and wore a lot of dark make up.

She instructed me to sit down in the first chair. I did and the guard came over and cuffed my legs to the bottom and both hands to the arms of the chair. The cuffs were actually built in to the chair so this must have been normal procedure. I suppose they wanted to be a little extra careful with prisoners so close to a pair of scissors.

She asked, "So, what do you want done?" I explained the hair cut I wanted the best I could and she replied, "You know, you're the first prisoner I've had that seems to care about their appearance. Most of 'em come in here and just say chop it all off. That cut would look good on you. You have a pretty face. Just stay away from the lesbians." She smiled with that comment. I smiled too. She seemed friendly and easy to talk to, unlike the guards. We talked a little as she cut my hair and the guard stood at the doorway waiting to take me back to my cell.

Once she was done, she held a mirror up to me so that I could see it. I couldn't believe how awesome it looked on me. She had actually done a wonderful job and I was pleased. I thanked her and the guard took the cuffs off of me to take me back to my cell.

As I was walking back to my cell, a few of the women commented through the bars at my haircut. "Hey Roxy! lookin' good." One of them said while another yelled, "Roxy, what's with the new look?" I felt good about my new hair style, which was what I probably needed. I had been losing my mind slowly in this place and had to do something for myself.

By the time I was back in my cell, I still had another hour before I had to go to work. I sat down at my desk and finally wrote the letter I had contemplated on writing. It only took me about forty five minutes to complete it, sealed it up in the envelope and give it to a guard. I felt confident about myself and had decided that I wouldn't put it off any longer. As I handed the completed letter over to the guard, he said, "This will go out with the mail tomorrow." I knew it would arrive within a few days after it was sent.

I felt lighter as I walked down to the laundry area to do my job. I was smiling more with my new look and felt confident for the first time in my life. There were still problems that I had to live with for the time, such as Shelly's group and Officer Wiley, but I knew it wouldn't last forever. Problems never do.

Kerry complimented my new haircut and we talked while we folded the clothes. Officer Yander never really harassed us about it much. He seemed to not care as long as we weren't causing trouble and we were getting our job done. When we would talk to each other, we'd always get more done than what was expected.

At dinner, Jaye and Denise also made comments about my new look. "You trying to get a new girlfriend?" Jaye asked as she smiled. I just smiled back. "Seriously, Roxy, it looks really good on you. You should keep it that way." Denise commented. I knew I would keep it short for a while. After dinner, we went to the showers where I was careful to avoid Shelly's friends and Officer Wiley. I had been careful anytime I was in any area where Shelly's group could attack me. Officer Wiley kept watching me from a distance.

After I was done with my shower and had gotten my shoes without any trouble from Shelly's friends, I felt someone grab my arm and pull me to the side. It was Officer Wiley and this time she looked as if she could rip my head off. She said, "I know all about you." I was confused but let her continue, "You think this haircut can make you seem more innocent? You were the one who killed that guard and I know it. They can't prove a thing but I just know it was you. It's always the innocent looking ones that are the most trouble."

That confirmed the fact that she definitely had it out for me but she had the wrong reasons. I wasn't even a part of the fight let alone had anything to do with killing the guard. "I kept my distance from the whole thing. I wasn't involved." I pleaded, but she wasn't buying it. "You would say that. I'm keeping a close watch on you and when you step out of line in the least little bit, I'll be there to put your ass in solitary for a month." She let my arm go and I joined in with the prisoners heading back upstairs to the cells.

As I sat in my cell that night, I thought about the obstacles I was facing and what I would do about it. I knew that something had to change but just wasn't sure how to change it. I contemplated on different options and none of them seemed feasible. I thought that maybe I could talk with Shelly and her friends like reasonable adults but dismissed that idea immediately. Shelly and her friends were not reasonable adults. They were animals as far as I could tell. They stared at me as if I were their prey and they hadn't eaten in over a month.

Then, I thought about Officer Wiley's threats and figured the only option I had was to file a complaint. I dismissed that idea as well because I had no idea whether or not I was even allowed to file a complaint on a guard. After all, I was the prisoner and had no rights.

Besides, the guards all seemed to stick together no matter what the situation so, if I were to make an issue out of the threat I had received, all the other guards would have joined in on the harassment. In addition, Officer Wiley seemed to be the Warden's favorite guard and I didn't need the Warden to gang up on me either. If I caused waves with the Warden, I would have definitely ended up in Cell Block D. After pondering my issues for some time, I finally fell asleep.

I woke up the next morning to the whistle and Officer Wiley standing right outside my cell. She was watching me like a hawk. I got up, dressed and began cleaning. I realized quickly that she was looking for one thing to punish me for. One wrong move was all it would take as she stared me down and she wasn't hiding it from anyone. It made me nervous knowing I had someone standing over my shoulder watching every move I made but I was careful to do everything correctly.

After breakfast, we went to our usual spot out in the courtyard and everyone started talking about their different issues. I didn't want to talk about my issues, since I realized there were no solutions to my problems. I didn't think the others would be able to come up with any ideas for me either.

Finally, Jaye said, "You're really quiet today, Roxy." "Not much to say, I guess." There was a moment of silence as they all wondered whether or not I was losing my mind but they eventually continued their conversations. I sat there quietly for the rest of our time outside.

We went to lunch and then headed off to work. I started walking out toward the cell blocks to meet up with my group when Officer Wiley stood in front of me and wouldn't let me pass. I argued, "I have to get to work." She gave a sinister smile and replied, "Your job assignment has changed." I just looked at her in disbelief as she continued, "I spoke to the Warden about you and gave him my opinion. He gave me the right to change your assignment. You're going to be on trash duty from now on."

I could feel my heart racing as I thought about trash duty and Shelly. She would be my co-worker once again. I knew that she wouldn't do anything to compromise her own well-being but I still felt uncomfortable with it. Plus, I knew that Officer Wiley was trying to get me in trouble. Perhaps she thought that I would attack Shelly. I reluctantly asked, "Who do I report to?"

"Me." I felt dizzy when I heard her say this. I tried my hardest to remain calm as I continued, "Where do we go for trash duty, Officer Wiley?" She began walking toward the back of the cafeteria and I followed. She instructed me to begin taking the trash bags out and place them into the big trash cart at the end of the cafeteria. With more than three hundred prisoners, I had a big job on my hands. There were at least fourteen trash cans in the main area and more than that in the kitchen.

I started working right away and was thankful that I hadn't seen Shelly. I finished putting all the bags in the bin and asked Officer Wiley what the next step was in the process. She instructed me to follow her through another door at the other end of the

178

cafeteria. This door led to a small caged area on the outside. There was a large black rimmed crater with smoke pouring out from it. Six other prisoners were working together to throw all the trash bags into this fire pit. They were sweating and the entire area stunk like rotting flesh. I could hardly breathe.

There were three guards standing around the prisoners and watching them closely. No one could talk to each other because they were too busy lifting heavy bags and passing them to the next prisoner in line as the last prisoner threw each one into the fire. Shelly was one of those prisoners. Officer Wiley shouted, "All of you will be pleased to know that Roxanne has brought you more work." All the prisoners began grunting and moaning at the sound of what she had said and I felt as if they truly were blaming me for having more trash to lift into the pit.

Officer Wiley then looked at me and snapped, "Get in line and do some work for once!" I stumbled over to the end of the line and began lifting the heavy bags. They must have weighed at least fifty pounds each, which wouldn't have been so bad if I only had to lift one. However, we had approximately three more hours to work with enough trash to last longer than that. I couldn't believe how my luck was just getting worse by the minute.

By the time we were finished and being taken to the cafeteria for dinner, I was exhausted. I could hardly lift my arms to pick up my tray and felt too tired to even be hungry. As soon as I sat down, everyone in my group backed away as they made comments about how horrible I smelled. "I was put on trash duty by Officer Wiley." I explained. Jaye looked at me and said, "What the hell did you do to get assigned to that? They usually keep that job for the trouble makers." I just gave her a look as if to say I already knew that.

"Officer Wiley is really mean. You should say something to someone about all this." Denise said. I was a little irritated by her comment and said, "Are you forgetting that we're in prison?! We don't have the right to say anything here." I could feel myself

179

getting angrier as I sat there thinking about how I was being treated and knowing I couldn't do a thing about it. Jaye added, "Plus, if you say anything, you'll just make it worse." I didn't know what to do about my situation but I had to do something.

That night after showers, I went back to my cell and thought more about the letter I had sent. I began to wonder if it would actually get to its destination. I had never sent a letter to anyone in my life prior to that one and was getting nervous that it would get lost.

Then, I realized that even if it did get to where it should go, it may just end up in the trash. What if she doesn't open it? Then, my hard work of coming up with the right words to say would be for nothing. I didn't want to dwell on the fact that my letter was probably written just to be tossed aside and ignored so I grabbed my book, laid down and read until I fell asleep.

I woke up that next morning with a deeper dread than I had ever had before. I guess it was brought on by knowing that I was on trash duty and my fate was in the hands of Officer Wiley, not to mention Shelly's group. After breakfast, I went to the courtyard and sat with my group on the bleachers and just listened to everyone else talk. I was so distressed with everything that I couldn't even join in with the conversations. I just sat there and stared back at Shelly and her group as they periodically stared at me. I couldn't take it anymore.

I stood up and walked over toward them. They all watched me as I came closer to them as if I were going to start something. I could hear Jaye right behind me as she tried desperately to stop me from whatever I was about to do. I knew in my mind that I was being irrational but I just couldn't take the harassment any longer. I walked right up to them and started yelling, "Do you have a problem with me? I'd like to know what it is! You're real good at throwing around empty threats but when it comes down to it, you're scared! Do something if you want to!"

Just then, a guard came running over and pulled me back as he said quietly in my ear, "You want to end up in solitary again? Don't let these women get to you." I was surprised to hear an Officer take my side. I felt like the world had been against me before hearing those words. I did as he said and backed off. As the guard began to lead me back to the bleachers, Shelly said, "Girl, it's enough to see you on trash duty everyday with me! Besides, I already kicked your ass once!"

I ignored the comment as I was led back to my place. The guard instructed me to not leave my spot until courtyard time was over. As I sat there, I began shaking as I tried my hardest to control my emotions. I could feel the tears coming but had to hold them back. People in prison don't cry, I kept telling myself. "Jaye, we need to do something." I said. "There's nothing we can do, Roxy!" Jaye snapped. "We are in prison. It's not supposed to be fun and games here! We're supposed to be harassed and thrown in cages. Society sees us as the animals we are!"

I didn't know how to respond to that so I stayed quiet and continued to force the tears back. "So, anyone hoping that we don't get meatloaf again tonight for dinner?" Denise said as she tried to change the conversation. She wasn't very effective at taking our minds off of the current situation.

We all yelled, "Shut up!" She hung her head and didn't say another word. Chris leaned over and patted my leg as she said, "You're going to be okay." She still seemed crazy even though she did speak once in a while. I was irritated by everything and chose not to respond even to her.

Then, I realized that out of all the ideas and solutions I had pondered, there was only one that would actually work to change my situation. I had been thinking about it periodically ever since Sarah had come to visit me. I suppose that was the last straw for me in prison and I had begun to ponder this new idea for a few days.

I said, "There is one thing we can do." Everyone looked at me eagerly waiting for me to finish. "We can break out of here." They all stared back at me in shock, obviously wondering if I was actually serious or not when the whistle blew.

# Chapter 19
# My Only Hope

After the whistle blew and we were herded back inside for lunch, we ate in silence. No one asked me about my comment on breaking out of prison and I assumed it was because they were afraid I was losing my mind. Maybe I was losing my mind but I knew deep down that I wouldn't be able to continue this way of life for much longer. At twenty six years old, I was not about to spend the rest of my life at Clausdrum.

After lunch, I remained in the cafeteria so I could report to Officer Wiley for my new job in trash duty. Once everyone else had cleared out of the cafeteria, Officer Wiley instructed me to gather up all the trash bags just as I had done the day before. I completed my task and obediently went outside to the incinerator with the other inmates on trash duty. As I lifted the fifty pound bags and handed them over to be thrown into the fire, I thought more about breaking out.

I realized that my mind was made up and I was going to leave Clausdrum no matter what the consequences. With each bag that I had to lift, I realized more and more that drowning in the freezing cold ocean would be better than this life. I was beginning to understand why the woman from solitary ripped her own arm open out of desperation to escape. I decided that I would escape whether any of my friends joined me or not.

Shelly continued to glare at me as I worked alongside all of the women. I began to get a little worried about whether or not I would survive this prison prior to my own escape. I had thought about my escape but I hadn't thought my plan through completely. I needed time to plan every detail. Even though no one else had successfully escaped by this point, I knew I had to make my best effort to get to the mainland and lose the police and tracking devices.

Once we were finished and one of the officers blew the whistle, I got in line with the other prisoners to go back inside for dinner. My stomach was growling with hunger after all the heavy work I had done. As I began walking toward the entrance to the cafeteria, I felt someone grab my arm and pull me out of the line. It was Officer Wiley. The other officer's stopped once they saw her grab me but she said, "I have this under control. I'll personally bring her inside after I have a talk with her about a matter that doesn't relate to any of you."

They quickly went back inside with the prisoners and left me outside alone with Officer Wiley. I had no idea what she could possibly want from me at this point. She had already been harassing me on a regular basis. She had made my life into a living hell and had nothing else to take away from me. I stood there shaking in my own shoes at the thought of what she might do next.

She was about two inches from my face as she growled, "You think I'm not on to you? You see those black boxes over there?" I looked and could see part of the courtyard from where I was standing and knew right away that she was talking about the recorder spies. Jaye had told me about those when I first arrived at the prison. However, Jaye had also theorized that the recorder spies that were in the area where we sat each day were spaced too far apart to pick up our voices.

My heart sank as I thought about where the conversation was going and realized that Officer Wiley must have heard me saying that I was planning to break out. I hadn't even been given the chance to try and escape and I was already going to face the consequences of it. My mind was racing on how I could possibly get out of this horrible mess I had caused, but I came up with nothing. I just nodded to Officer Wiley to let her know I could see the little black boxes.

She continued, "Well, I've heard the other inmates talking about you and how you were responsible for the fight that broke out. If you were responsible for rallying the other prisoners to attack the guards, then that must mean you're responsible for the death of the officer that night. I'm holding it against you and if I can prove it, you're going to Cell Block D." I gave a huge sigh of relief at those words. I thought that perhaps Shelly and her group had been trying to set me up by saying that I was behind the fight. They probably knew about the recorder spies as well.

I knew I wasn't guilty of the huge prison fight that had occurred and realized that there would be no way she could pin it on me. I also realized that Jaye had been right about the recorder spies we sat next to everyday. If Officer Wiley had been listening to the conversations from the courtyard, she definitely would have heard me say that I wanted to break out of prison. That would have been a serious offense as far as the guards were concerned, especially after two failed attempts just recently.

She let me go and I went inside to get my dinner. I was still shaking slightly but tried my hardest to hide it from anyone around me. After I had gotten my dinner tray and sat down, the others had already been seated and were waiting for the whistle to blow. We started eating but no one said a word to me about my earlier comment on escaping.

"So, Denise, how did you do with your job today?" Jaye asked. I was confused by the question. "I did okay, but I almost 'broke out' into a sweat." Jaye looked at me as soon as Denise had

185

said this. I knew right away that they were trying to tell me something but I had no idea what. Jaye continued, "Did you have a good lunch today, Kerry?"

"No, I kept 'breaking' all my plastic forks." I was still struggling to catch on when Chris spoke up, "I don't want to break my leg tomorrow or the next day." I was beginning to understand when Jaye said, "Well, I'll take that risk. Maybe we can talk more about it tomorrow."

They had been speaking in a sort of code to tell me that they were all willing to at least listen to my plan and work with me on it, except for Chris. She had caught on to the secret language before I did and had obviously expressed that she wanted no parts of it. That made sense to me since she is crazy and seems to feel safe in prison. It was the only life she knew. I didn't think Chris would have had a chance at survival on the outside. She had been a prisoner since the age of eighteen and was probably crazy prior to that.

After dinner and showers, I went back to my cell and thought more about how to break out of prison. I already had an idea and knew the weakness that had prevented anyone from escaping so I continued to build on that. The microchips were the biggest problem in preventing prisoners from actually succeeding in their attempts at freedom.

I had learned before that there was a computer room where the prison guards would track the location of every prisoner at all times. If a prisoner was not in the place where they should be, guards would be released into that area to track them down. No one could escape as long as they had that microchip.

By eliminating the microchips, a prisoner would actually have a chance at escape. Of course that led me to brainstorm on how to get rid of the microchips. They are small and located in the upper left arm. Our microchips had been a part of our own bodies since we were born. Everyone had one inserted just after birth. The only way to get rid of them is to cut them out.

As soon as I realized that this was the first step in the escape plan, I wondered if the others would back out. We would have to get supplies somehow in order to remove the chips but I wasn't sure how we would manage that. None of us, except for Chris, worked in the kitchen and that was the only place I knew of that had access to small knives. Chris had said she was on dish duty so it was a possibility that she could get pairing knives. But, I wasn't sure if they kept a count of how many they had and whether or not Chris could pull that off.

I figured that if I thought about it long enough, I'd come up with some way of removing the microchips. I cringed at the thought but I was willing to dig my arm open with my own nails if I had to. The other problem I ran into with eliminating the microchips was that we would probably bleed a lot and it would be difficult to hide that from the guards and other prisoners. We would have to get access to tape or something to keep the wounds closed until we could get to the mainland.

I figured as soon as our microchips were gone, we could then hide them somewhere in the cafeteria during one of the mealtimes and sneak out toward the front entrance. When I had been taken to the hospital, I noticed that the hallway toward that area along with the front of the prison was not guarded during dinner time. I assumed it was because of the fact that all the prisoners were in the cafeteria and the microchips would be tracked if they weren't.

If we were to leave our microchips somewhere in the cafeteria, none of the guards would be signaled to look for us anywhere else. Plus, the cafeteria is hectic and busy as the prisoners get their food and settle into a seat. The guards wouldn't even notice that we were gone.

Once we were past the guards and through the front entrance, we could take one of the floaters to the mainland without being seen. The sun sets just after dinner is served and we would definitely have a chance at not being seen once we crossed the ocean to the other side. It would be dark enough by the time we arrived on the mainland so that no one would see us walking around in our yellow jumpsuits.

I was excited as I thought more about my plan and tried to find ways around the flaws. I knew that I would come up with some way of getting rid of the microchips since I was desperate enough. I also felt confident that one of the others may have some ideas as well. We also had to figure out how everyone would survive without a microchip once we got to the mainland. I didn't want to have to kill innocent people just to steal their identities.

Besides, there were too many flaws in that plan as it was. If the police found bodies and then saw that their bank accounts had being accessed, they'd easily track us by the stolen identities and bring us back to prison. The only way to successfully live off of someone else's microchip would be to go on a lifetime killing spree, constantly changing the microchip.

That wasn't feasible at all in my opinion. We had to think it through a little more before carrying out the first step in our plan. I wanted the escape to be perfect from the very beginning so that we wouldn't run into problems later on.

I fell asleep a little while after thinking more on the ideas I had and dreamed again about my freedom. I was swimming toward the mainland in my dream with no officers or police tracking me. There were no Mini Sirens or computers locked into my microchip. I looked at my arm and saw a small incision that was neatly stitched up and healing. I got the other side with a new identity.

When I woke up to the whistle, I thought to myself how nice it would be if things were as easy as my dreams. I realized my plan had many flaws and I had no idea how to get past them. I cleaned my cell and headed to breakfast wondering if the others would have any ideas to overcome the obstacles that were obvious in the escape plan. Maybe they would be able to think through it better than I could and would come up with a way to get rid of the chips and survive on the other side.

I knew I would be able to survive. I had always been a survivor. However, I was more worried about their survival without a microchip. They had all volunteered to join me in the escape and were willing to help in any way they could to make this a success. I wanted to be sure they were going be okay once we were free again.

As we ate our breakfast, none of us really spoke much at all. We were all eager to get outside and brain storm a little more on our plan. But, we forced ourselves to wait until we were outside in our place where we wouldn't be heard. After knowing that Jaye was right about the recorder spies not picking up our voices, I wasn't as afraid about speaking to the others and planning the prison break.

We had three hours to come up with the perfect plan and I knew that we would have to carry it out and escape in no more than two weeks. I was just hoping that the others would be willing to escape that soon and not ask too many questions as to why. I needed to escape this life as soon as I possibly could.

Once we were outside and all seated on the bleachers, Jaye was the first one to speak up. "So, what's our plan?" "The first thing we have to do is get rid of our microchips but I don't know how." I replied. "I know how." Jaye said. We all looked at her and she continued, "Are you all forgetting that I work with the Nurse?" "The Nurse will cut them out for us?" Denise asked with surprise. I just shook my head at her stupidity.

"No, she won't but I have access to supplies and I know how to use them. I've seen her stitch people up plenty of times and

189

I can teach you." Jaye was right about having access to the supplies but I wasn't convinced that we would know what to do once we got them. "Are we going to do surgery on each other?" I asked. "Not on each other. That would be too risky. Someone would see us. No, we have to each do surgery on ourselves discreetly, in the privacy of our own cells."

"Is that going to be too hard for us to learn?" Kerry asked. "It may be a little messy but it's just like sewing. I can get us each a scalpel, stitching thread and needles and gauze. Just cut a smooth straight line across your arm, reach in, take the chip out and then sew it back up with the needle and thread."

Kerry looked a little worried, "What if we cut in the wrong place?" "You won't. If you grab your arm where the fatty part is and squeeze a little, you can feel the microchip." Everyone started grabbing their own arms instinctively. "Not here! The guards will get suspicious." Jaye said. We all stopped and continued to try and be less conspicuous.

"Once you find the small hard area, you know where to cut. We have to do this discreetly and stop when the guards come around to walk past your cell. I can get plenty of gauze and tape as well, so that we can keep our jumpsuits from getting any blood on them." We all agreed that this would be a good idea. We certainly didn't want to draw any attention to ourselves and agreed that we had to be extremely careful with the entire process.

I was glad Jaye had come up with a way to get rid of the microchips but I knew that was only the beginning of the plan. Apparently, I wasn't the only one who was eager to know the plan in its entirety. Denise asked, "What do we do after that?"

I replied this time, "We have to throw the guards off by keeping the microchips on us at all times until we're ready to actually leave." "So, then what do we do with our microchips when we're ready to leave?" Denise inquired. I continued to explain, "I was thinking that we could leave just as dinner is being served. All

190

the guards will be focused on the prisoners in the cafeteria during that time. We can toss our microchips somewhere to throw the computers off and slip out through the chaos so that the guards don't see us either."

"We can throw the microchips in the trash can right by the entrance to the cafeteria. We won't even have to go into the cafeteria to get to that trash can." Jaye mentioned. She was starting to sound rather excited that the plan was coming together. Denise still seemed a little concerned about the details of the plan by that point.

I continued to explain the rest of the plan, "Once we're past the guards and ditch our microchips, we can go through the hall that passes by the visitors station and right out through the main entrance. There are no guards in that hallway and as long as they think were in the cafeteria, they won't have any reason to patrol that area of the prison."

"It's all coming together. I like it so far." Kerry said. "After we get outside, we can take one of the floaters to the mainland. They keep at least two of them out front and there are no fences." Denise seemed to become more and more worried about every detail as we spoke. "Are the floaters safe? Does anyone know how to drive one? I can't swim." "Don't worry about swimming. You won't have to, Denise. Just don't fall off the floater." Jaye said.

I realized that I had more questions as well. "What is everyone going to do when we reach the mainland?" I asked. "I don't know. I guess we'll figure it out once we get over there." Jaye said. Kerry intervened with an idea, "We could live off of the land. Does anyone know how to grow fruit?" We all gave her a blank look. "That's what I thought. I can't grow anything either" Kerry said as she realized her idea wouldn't work.

"What about fake microchips?" Denise said. It was the first time throughout the entire conversation that she had said something productive. "And where do we get fake microchips?"

Jaye asked. "I know a person who has access to the place where they make microchips. They're blank at first but he can add anything to it. He can get fake identities. Then, wire the information into the fake chips and we have new accounts." It made sense and everyone else seemed to like the idea.

"Well, we have to have this done in two weeks." I said. Everyone looked at me and Jaye asked, "Why two weeks? You got a date or something?" I explained, "No, I just can't stay here longer than that." I didn't say anything else about it and everyone seemed content with leaving as soon as possible.

"How soon can you get us the supplies we need?" I asked. Jaye said, "Give me a few days. I can't take all of it at once for obvious reasons. I'll take a few here and there and once we have everything we need, we can plan a night to cut our microchips out and escape the day after."

I was beginning to feel anxious not knowing if we would be able to pull this plan off in such a short amount of time but I had to trust that Jaye would get us the supplies with time to spare. I still wanted to convince them on the importance of getting out of prison within that time frame. "Okay, let's plan on breaking out of here the Friday after next, at dinner time." I figured that if they had an actual deadline, they would work a little harder to reach that goal. Everyone nodded and Jaye said, "I can get the supplies by the end of this week so that shouldn't be a problem at all."

We all sat there for a few moments taking in everything we had discussed. Then, Jaye said, "So, next Friday. That's fourteen days away if you count today. Is there something you want to tell us, Roxy?" She still didn't trust me on my reasoning for wanting to be free in two weeks.

She was becoming more and more suspicious. I became defensive as I answered, "I just can't take it any longer and I need to get out of here as soon as we can. I know that our plan will take time but it shouldn't take longer than that. It's just a suggestion, Jaye."

She didn't say anything else about it after that. I guess she believed my reasoning which helped me to relax about the whole thing a little more. It was enough that we rarely ever trusted each other but to act as if I had something big to hide was too much for me to handle. I knew we had to remain focused on the escape and trust issues could easily hinder us.

Everyone else in my group didn't seem to feel as distrusting as Jaye but I realized I shouldn't have snapped. I really didn't want Jaye to back out of the plan so I tried to smooth things over. "I'm sorry. I just need to get out of here before Shelly and her group attack me again. Plus, I'm on trash duty. Do you realize how hard that is?"

Jaye seemed to understand and apologized as well. We decided that we would do everything possible to make sure our plan went through without any problems or suspicions. Each day for the next week, Jaye would get a few supplies at a time. We would get them from her in any place where we could discreetly exchange supplies and tuck them into our clothing.

The first day she had supplies for us was a Monday. She had gotten them the previous Saturday, which was also the day we had discussed our plan. I was in line for breakfast when she came up behind me and nudged my arm.

I saw what she was doing right away and took the small scalpel from her. It had a hard piece of plastic over the blade so it was safe to put it in my shoe without cutting myself. I purposely dropped my fork and when I bent down to pick it up, I slipped the little knife in.

The second day, she slipped a handful of gauze and chlorhexidine packets to me. She explained that the small purple packets were for cleaning the area prior to making the cut in the skin and that it would prevent any infection. I reminded her that we would be swimming across an ocean with fresh wounds on our arms and that it didn't seem to matter much if we got an infection from the actual incision. She just shook her head and smiled. I took the little packet anyway.

On Tuesday, she gave me a syringe with medication in it. I asked her, "What's in the syringe?" She replied, "It's Lidocaine and it will numb your arm up before you go cutting into yourself." That made sense so I hid it in the top portion of my jumpsuit. She also brought me a needle with some thread that had a tough texture to it. It seemed to be strong enough to keep a deep wound closed at least temporarily depending on how well the knot is.

She would always bring us the supplies early in the day so that we could take them back to our cells prior to lunch. We would take turns requesting to go to the prison store and buy small items that didn't cost much. Once we were taken back to our cells to drop the items off, we would sneak the items that Jaye had given us into our cells with the items we had bought from the store. The guards didn't seem to suspect a thing.

Everything was going smoothly and right on schedule. I was actually getting more nervous about how well things were going than I was about the actual escape. It just didn't feel right to me that things should be going as smoothly as they were. I had a dreaded feeling that anything could go wrong at any moment and the whole plan would be ruined. I tried not to think about it too much and just focused my energy on each step of the plan and lifting those heavy bags during work hours.

The only good thing that came from being transferred to trash duty was the fact that I was feeling stronger each day. With all the lifting I was doing for four hours straight with no breaks, I was gaining muscle. I knew that would help me in my escape plan since it would take skill and strength to pull it off.

I figured that if we did make it to the floater, we would still run the risk of having to swim. I refused to share this information with Denise, who was still afraid that she could drown. She continued to get more worried everyday about crossing the ocean and continued to remind us that she couldn't swim. We just continued to reassure her that she wouldn't have to as long as she stayed on the floater, which was true.

Each night when I was sent back to my cell, I would take the supplies Jaye had given me that day and put them in my mattress. The guards hadn't seen any of the things we were going to be using in our escape plan and we did everything we could to make sure they never did. We were going to escape and we weren't planning on getting caught. As far as I could tell, we had the perfect escape plan.

# Chapter 20
# Microchips

Over the course of the next few days, we spoke very little about the plan to escape only because of the fear of being caught. Everyone was getting a little nervous about it and we were slightly on edge. When we did speak about it, we only did so in order to clarify the plan so that everyone in our group knew exactly what to do. Jaye went over the process again of how to remove the microchip and stitch the area.

At night, while I was in my cell alone, I would reach around my upper arm and squeeze the fatty area that contained the microchip. I could feel it. It was a small square area that was slightly harder than the rest of my arm. I would have guessed that the microchip was no bigger than the end of my finger. I couldn't imagine how it could possibly hold as much information as it did.

On Thursday morning, after breakfast, we all congregated to our usual spot in the courtyard, two weeks after we had initially spoke about our escape plan. As we sat there together, I could feel the tension in the air around us as everyone silently dreaded the coming day that we would carry out such a risky plan. "We're going tomorrow, right?" I asked everyone. The others nodded and

Kerry commented, "I guess so. We have everything we need and the plan is set. There's no reason why we wouldn't."

"Maybe we should rethink this again. Is there any other way to get to the mainland that doesn't involve crossing the water? I can't swim." Denise said in a worried voice. "You won't have to swim. How many times do we have to tell you? Just stay on the boat." Jaye said. Denise had been getting more and more worried as the days went on. She kept thinking that she'd have to swim and was convinced she wasn't going to survive the escape.

"We have gone over it several times. The guards aren't going to know we're gone so they won't be looking for us." I reassured her. "See that tower up there?" Jaye asked. Denise looked up toward the tower and nodded.

"They have computers in there that track our microchips and officers are watching the screens constantly. If someone is not where they're supposed to be, then they sound a signal to the other guards. If we leave our microchips in the cafeteria and leave through the front entrance, they'll never see us. Therefore, we take the floater and head toward the mainland on a nice quiet boat ride."

Jaye was good at explaining things to make them simple to understand. Denise seemed to feel much better after Jaye had explained the computers and why the plan would work. However, she was still certain that she would fall off of the boat. We continued to reassure her that she wouldn't because Jaye had driven a boat before she was sentenced to prison. She had no experience with a floater, of course, which is slightly different than a Bay Liner, but she did have experience with a boat none the less.

Even I was slightly nervous about the entire plan. Even though I felt rather confident about the actual escape, I was more afraid of what might happen on the mainland. I didn't know if we'd all be able to survive without our microchips. I had had mine since I was born. We all did.

197

Removing it was much like removing my own heart. As far as I could remember, the microchip was my life line with getting food, shelter, jobs and anything else I needed. I couldn't live without it. I was certain that I would get another one with a different name and identification, but I still felt a sense of sadness at losing the one I was given when I was born.

"So, when you get back to your cells tonight, start cutting the microchip out immediately. Don't wait too long to do it because you don't know how long it'll take. There's tissue grown in around it and it might be hard to remove. Plus, you have to stop every time you see a guard come by your cell." Jaye reminded us. We all knew this information already because she had reminded us each day. Even though she didn't show it, I believe Jaye was nervous as well.

After we went back inside, ate our lunch and reported to our jobs, I kept thinking about the escape that would happen in twenty four hours. As Officer Wiley shouted orders at me and Shelly continued to glare, I knew I was making the right decision. The more I lifted those heavy bags and built up my muscles, the more confident I was in my plan. Everything had been well thought out and the plan was not created by someone who had lost their mind.

The other inmates had tried to escape but they weren't patient enough to really overcome every obstacle. They had attempted their escaped primarily because they couldn't take one more day. I reasoned with myself on it. Compared to a lifetime, what's two more weeks? I had thought to myself about the freedom I would have as I continued to sweat from the hard labor they had me doing. The only thing that kept me going was the knowledge that it would be my second to last day on trash duty.

Once our four hours of torture was over and we were to go back inside for dinner and showers, I was starving. I sat down and waited for the whistle to blow and just stared back at the rest of the people in my group. Their faces were looking a little less than confident about the plan. I knew they were just nervous because of

198

the fact that the other prisoners had just attempted an escape and failed. We weren't going to fail.

We didn't speak much during our meal and I noticed that the guard that always stood by our table seemed to be watching us with suspicion. I realized right away that our silence and tension was causing him to believe that something was wrong. I spoke up right away, "So, Jaye, hear any news lately on Shelly's group?" I had to say something and that's all I could come up with. Jaye understood what I was thinking and jumped right in, "Nope. Not a word. I think they finally got the hint that we're not to be messed with."

Everyone, including the guards, knew that Shelly's group had been harassing me every day since my arrival to Clausdrum so this happened to be a good cover up story to hide our thoughts about the escape. "That's good." I responded. "I have a funny story to tell." Denise said.

We all listened knowing that any conversation would lead the guard to believe that everything was normal. "When we were cleaning the bathrooms today, one of the girls slipped on the wet floor and knocked over a bucket. She wasn't happy about it." The story wasn't funny at all in my opinion but I was glad to see that the guard had turned his attention away from us when the tension had died down.

When dinner was over and we had taken our trays to the drop off area, we waited to go downstairs to the showers. Things seemed to be going according to plan but I was getting more nervous about cutting into my own arm. I had only an hour before I would have to perform the surgery on myself. I did my best to not think about it and just focus on each minute of the day as I went through my normal routines.

Once I was done getting my shower, the guard gave me two clean jumpsuits and I couldn't help but think to myself how pointless it was for me to have so many when I wasn't going to be in prison anymore. I went into the changing room to get dressed and then get my shoes. I began to walk out into the hallway when I saw Shelly and her group being led down toward the showers. I held my breath as they all stared back at me. I didn't understand why, but I had a bad feeling about it.

I only had to avoid them for one more day and then I'd never have to see any of them again. Maybe it was the way they were staring or the manner in which they walked toward me but I had a dreaded feeling about them that I hadn't felt since Shelly had attacked me. I froze in the doorway to try and avoid them but was shoved from behind as a woman said, "Move out of my way! I'd like to get back to my cell now!"

I was pushed forward though the doorway and into the hallway as Shelly's group was right out in front of the changing room. Shelly smiled and I saw a fist from one of her friends coming right for me. Everything seemed to move in slow motion as I ducked out of the way.

Just as I ducked and stepped forward under her arm, I heard her fist make contact with someone. The woman from behind me who had shoved me out of the room had been hit in the face by Shelly's friend. I turned around just in time to see the woman hit her back. I jumped out of the way and scurried past the crowd of prisoners that was quickly forming around the fighting women.

As I was heading toward the stairs to go back to my cell, guards were running in the opposite direction to break up the fight. I couldn't get upstairs and away from the action fast enough. If I had gotten hit, I would have gone to solitary confinement. I would have lost the chance for escaping this prison.

As I thought about how lucky I had been, I wondered if the others would have continued with the plan without me. I was hoping that I would never have to find out the answer to that question. I was just glad to have avoided the obstacle and hoped that I would continue to be so lucky throughout the next day.

Once I was in my cell again, I let out a huge sigh of relief and sat down on my bed. There were no guards around my cell so I took out the supplies Jaye had given me over the last week. I had my pajamas on and the material was much softer than the jumpsuits so I was able to reach my upper arm easily without having to undress. I slid my right arm out of the sleeve and into the pajamas so that I could reach my left arm in order to perform the surgery.

I began to sweat as I thought about what I was doing. I closed my eyes and thought back to what Jaye had told us. She had given us step by step instructions on how to do the surgery. I took a deep breath and forced myself to begin whether I wanted to or not.

I took the handful of gauze and lined my pajamas with it just around the area I was planning on cutting. Then, I took the chlorhexidine out of the small package and used it to wipe the area for a couple of minutes to ensure that it was clean. A guard walked by my cell and I closed my eyes as I leaned against the wall. I could hear the footsteps stop right in front of my cell. I opened my eyes to peer out and saw the guard standing there peering back at me.

"Long day." I said. He grunted and continued on his way. Then, I took the syringe that Jaye had given me and started to stab myself with it but hesitated. The top half of my pajamas was large enough to allow me to see my left arm where I was to do the surgery but I was afraid that I was too exposed to the guards. If I were to start cutting and I guard walked by, I wouldn't be able to stop the bleeding right away and the guard would see that I had been cutting myself.

I decided it would probably be best if I laid down on my side with my left arm leaning on the pillow. I laid down and pulled the blanket over my head. There wasn't much light but I had to make do with it since I didn't want to get caught. I had the needle and I knew about where the microchip was located so I stabbed my

201

arm. The needle was large and it hurt but I gritted my teeth and began injecting the Lidocaine into my skin.

I waited a few minutes until the numbing took full effect and then I grabbed hold of the scalpel. My hands were shaking by this point but I knew I had no other choice. I figured either I was going to escape or I was going to die trying. I took the plastic sleeve off of the sharp knife and barely touched my skin with the blade. I was already bleeding. I had no choice but to keep going at this point.

I cut in a little deeper and found that the Lidocaine had numbed the area completely. I felt no pain as I dug the knife in and pulled it across the skin. I made a clean straight cut just over the area where the microchip was located. I looked closer and saw that I still had not cut deep enough. I couldn't see the microchip. The gauze was soaking up the blood and I knew I had to move faster.

I went back over the same cut again but the Lidocaine only went so deep. I could feel the second cut. I continued despite the pain as I gritted my teeth even harder. As I pulled the knife across the cut, the blade hit something hard.

It was the microchip. I put the knife aside and reached my fingers into the wound as far as I could to grab the small chip. I could reach it but had trouble grabbing it. I managed to latch on to the edge of it with two fingers but could feel the pain and pressure the further I reached into the wound.

My fingers were slippery but I held on to the microchip as tightly as I could as I pulled it outward. I peeked at my arm just as I had the microchip at the surface and saw that there was fatty tissue wrapped all around the actual chip. I couldn't let go of the microchip or it would snap back inside the wound so I pulled as hard as I could. I only had one hand to work with and couldn't use the knife to cut away the extra tissue. I had no choice but to rip the tissue away from the chip.

I continued to pull as the pain became almost unbearable. Just as I thought I would pass out, the microchip broke away from the skin. I had pulled it out. I stuffed it under my pillow and grabbed the last of the supplies I needed. I had to stitch up the wound. I was able to use both hands to thread the small needle but I had to hurry before the gauze pads were completely soaked in blood.

Once I had the needle threaded and was back into the side laying position, I made the first stitch. The Lidocaine was still working to keep the outer layers of skin numbed and stitching the wound wasn't nearly as bad as the first part of the procedure. I was able to stitch the wound closed without any problems at all. The skin was cut smoothly and went back together with very little bleeding. I took the remaining gauze and cleaned the blood off of the area.

My microchip was out and my identity was gone. I knew that the very next day I would have a new identity and have the chance at living life again as a free person. I figured there would be sacrifices to make in order to gain that freedom but I would be free again no matter what the cost. I laid awake for most of the night as I thought about my freedom. Eventually, I fell asleep and dreamed about it.

The next morning I awoke to the piercing sound of the whistle and I quickly reminded myself that it would be the last time I'd ever have to wake up to that awful sound again. I checked my arm and found that it was not bleeding. Then, I cleaned my room and check my arm again. I was beginning to panic at the thought that the stitches wouldn't hold. I was checking my arm before and after each assignment. I got dressed and then checked for bleeding once again.

I had my microchip under my pillow the entire night while I slept. After I was dressed, I discreetly slipped the microchip into the top portion of my jumpsuit. The waist of my jumpsuit was elastic, which was form fitting around the middle, so the microchip was secure inside. No guards had seen me take the microchip out and put it in my clothes so I knew I was safe.

Once we were in the cafeteria, I couldn't wait see how surgery went with the others. I sat down across from Kerry and asked, "So, did you get your work done yesterday?" I tried to be subtle with my question so that we wouldn't tip the guards off about our plan. "Yes, but I had a lot of trouble." She seemed concerned so I told her we would talk once we got outside.

Denise and Jaye joined us only moments later and said nothing about the microchips. I realized that I shouldn't have asked Kerry about it until we were outside so I remained quiet during the remainder of our meal time. We spoke about other things instead. Jaye asked, "Did you guys hear about the fight in the showers yesterday?" Denise and Kerry had already gone up to their cells before I did so they hadn't seen it.

They both said no and I began filling them in on the details. "Apparently, one of Shelly's friends got into a fight. She was actually swinging at me but missed and hit another woman. I slipped out before seeing how bad it got." Jaye added, "I was behind you in taking my shower so I saw the whole thing. It was intense. Shelly's friend got her ass kicked. There was blood everywhere by the time the guards broke it up."

I was glad it was someone else other than me involved in that fight. Jaye continued, "I didn't know that she was trying to hit you. I didn't see that part of it." "I ducked." We started laughing and couldn't stop. The guards began giving us scowled looks but we just couldn't control ourselves. Perhaps it was a combination of the stress from being in prison while planning to break out and the fact that the story truly was that funny.

Eventually, our laughter died down as breakfast came to an end and we went outside for our courtyard time. Shelly's group had one less member in it that morning and the ones that were left standing by the basketball courts continued with their glaring as they whispered to each other. I was hoping they weren't planning on starting anything soon since I was trying so hard to fly under the radar. I had to go through with the escape plan and didn't want any of them to ruin it for me.

"I couldn't get the stitches on right." Kerry continued what she had been complaining about when we were inside. "At first it wouldn't lace right and then I couldn't tie the knot. I only had one hand. How do you tie a knot with one hand?" She was looking worried about the work she had done on her arm and she couldn't show us without the guards noticing. "As long as it's not bleeding, you'll be fine." Jaye said. "I tied mine using my teeth along with my one free hand. If you make the thread so that one side is really long then you can do that." Denise added.

"I assume that everyone has their microchips on them since there are no guards chasing us." Jaye added. "We all have them." We said. "Good. Are they in a place where you can get to them easily? We'll need to ditch them at dinner but we don't want to look suspicious." Denise looked away as she said, "I have mine in my shoe. I guess I should move it then." She got up and requested to use the public bathroom so that she could have privacy as she found another place to put the microchip.

"I just don't get her sometimes." I said. Everyone seemed to agree as we continued to talk about Denise's lack of common sense. We then went back through the plan again to make sure everyone knew what to do. "The next step is to ditch the chips. We need to put them in the trash right next to the door to the cafeteria so we can slip out unnoticed." Jaye said. "I think we should stagger in separately so that the guards don't see us all together in a group looking suspicious." Kerry added.

"That's a really good idea. I hadn't thought of that." I commented. Chris spoke up at that point. I had almost forgotten she was with us since she was so quiet all the time. "It's a good plan. You're going to be free today." Just then, Denise came walking back to the bleachers. She had moved her microchip to her jumpsuit so that she could reach it easily when it came time to ditch the chip.

I took what Chris said to heart and believed that we would succeed in our plan. Kerry and Jaye felt the same way I did but Denise was still worrying about every detail. "So, if we stagger in, then where should we meet?" She asked. "We'll meet up in the hallway toward the front entrance." I answered.

Jaye continued, "Then, we go from there to the shoreline where we board one of the floaters. It can't be that hard to figure out how to use one." I added, "Then, we get to the mainland from there." Everyone seemed to feel a little better since we had gone over the plan once again. Not one of us could come up with a single flaw, especially after our microchips were removed.

The whistle blew and we headed back inside for lunch. As I sat down and stared at my stale chicken sandwich and glass of water, I realized that this would be my last meal before attempting to escape. Either I would be dead before my next meal or I would be sitting down with a juicy steak before the day was over. I just knew that I was not going to eat prison food again. I would escape or I would die trying.

# Chapter 21
# The Chase

As I sat there waiting for everyone to get their food and sit down, I heard someone from the lunch line yell, "You have blood all over you!" I checked my arm. It wasn't bleeding so I turned around to where the woman was standing and I saw Kerry with blood saturating her sleeve.

Everyone was staring at her as she stared back in horror at the knowledge that she had been caught. Guards came rushing over toward her and led her out of the cafeteria. She looked back at me as they escorted her away and I could see the terror in her eyes. My heart sunk as I thought about what might happen to her.

I knew she wasn't going to be escaping with the rest of us but I wondered if the other remaining two would be brave enough to continue with the plan. "I don't think we'll be seeing Kerry again." Jaye said as she walked over to the table to sit down. "Are we going to continue?" I asked.

"I don't see why we shouldn't. In fact, now we have more reason to go through with it. She might sell us out before the end of the day. So, we have to get out of here." Jaye said quietly. With all the commotion around us, the guards couldn't hear us talking. I looked around to make sure that no one else had heard but everyone seemed to be preoccupied with the incident involving Kerry.

I turned back around in my seat and waited for the whistle to blow. We ate our food in silence as we all worried about Kerry and wondered whether or not she would sell us out. We had to move fast and stay on schedule with the plan. It was possible that Kerry would keep our secret but none of us had any way of knowing for sure.

After lunch, I remained in the cafeteria and obediently did as Officer Wiley instructed me to. I worked harder at trash duty than I had ever worked before. I worked out of fear mostly since I didn't want to stir up any trouble this close to escaping. I had dodged a fight the night before and I wasn't about to give Officer Wiley any reason to detain me.

I knew that I had to be on my best behavior at this point so that she had no reason to keep me from carrying out my plan. Once I was outside with the other prisoner's, I worked harder than the rest of them. With every bag I lifted, I thought about the muscle I had gained over the last couple of weeks.

Trash duty ended up being a blessing for me and would be useful in my plan. I knew that I had to be strong in order to escape. There was always the chance that we would have to swim, despite what we had told Denise. Denise continued to worry about the possibility of having to swim in the ocean. I figured that if anything did happen and she fell off the boat, I'd go after her.

I had always been a good swimmer and now that I was feeling stronger and more confident, I was sure that I'd have no problem with fighting the currents and the freezing waters. I would protect Denise but she had trouble trusting that she would be safe during the escape. Even if Denise did drown in the ocean, at least she would be free in a way. Plus, I reminded myself that the only person that mattered was me.

I wasn't worried about Jaye. I knew that Jaye was even more of a survivor than I was. She was bigger and naturally stronger than me. She had spent more than ten years surviving this prison and I knew that she would have no trouble at all with surviving the escape. Nothing could bring that woman down and I knew it. I assumed that if any one of us was to die during this venture, it would be Denise and not Jaye.

The four hours of work went by quickly and before I knew it the whistle blew. We all lined up to go back inside for dinner. In our case, we would go back inside to escape Clausdrum. My heart was racing so fast I could hardly breathe as I filed back into the cafeteria with the rest of the prisoners. Officer Wiley was right behind me as we walked in. I was nervous that she wouldn't leave my side.

Once we were inside again, I stood there at the back doorway where I had come in from and I saw Jaye. She was standing at the entrance to the cafeteria on the other side. Denise was standing about ten feet away from her at the entrance as well looking nervous. Jaye looked over at me and nodded, then went to the trash can at the doorway and stood in front of it. She had her hand discreetly behind her back.

I glanced behind to see if Officer Wiley was still standing there but she was gone. She had slipped through the crowd and disappeared among the chaos of the prisoners getting their meals. I scanned the room looking for her. I had to know where she was before I made my move. I spotted her on the other side of the large room talking with another Officer. They walked out of the cafeteria together.

I looked back over to find Jaye but she was gone. She must have slipped out as well toward the front entrance of the prison. Denise was still standing at the entrance looking lost and confused as she waited for someone to tell her what to do next. I made my way over to her and pretended I was getting in line for my meal.

I leaned in and said, "Wait two minutes, then ditch the chip and meet us in the hall." She heard me and stayed right where she was as I walked nonchalantly toward the trash can. I stood behind two prisoners that were standing in front of the trash can. I had pulled my microchip out of the top portion of my jumpsuit and had it in my hand. I made sure no one was looking in my direction and then slipped the microchip into the trash can. It landed on top of the trash where it could be seen, so I reached in and pulled a napkin over the chip so that it wasn't obvious.

Then, I looked around once again and slipped out of the cafeteria toward the hallway to the main entrance. There were no guards around since they all thought we were still in the cafeteria with the others. Our plan was working so far.

I met up with Jaye and we just stood there in the hallway as we waited for the last member of our party to join us. "I told her to wait two minutes so that we didn't look suspicious." I explained. Jaye nodded but was beginning to look nervous as well. We stood there in silence for three minutes. There was no sign of Denise.

Another minute had gone by and Jaye was getting more fidgety. She said, "We give her one more minute and then we leave." I agreed. She could have been caught and if that were the case, we would be caught as well. If they saw her microchip was gone, they would rush her past the very spot we were standing in to take her to the hospital. That would ruin the entire plan.

I was also concerned about Kerry. I hadn't seen her since she was taken away earlier that day. I wondered if they were interrogating her and trying to make her tell of the plan and who was involved. I knew we had to hurry and Jaye seemed to feel the same way.

"Okay, we've waited long enough. Let's get going." Jaye said. We started to head off toward the entrance when Denise came rushing around the corner to meet up with us. "Why did it take you so long?" I asked. "Sorry. A guard came around and stood at the trash can by the door to the cafeteria. I didn't think I was going to make it but he finally moved."

I began to wonder if it was a good idea to include Denise in our plan but it was already done. The three of us rushed down the hallway, around the corner and to the front entrance. Once we were at the doors to the prison, we opened the door slowly in order to not make any sound.

The three of us peeked out through the doorway to make sure there was no one around. When we didn't see a single guard, we made our next move. We ran outside and hid behind another building that was closer to the shoreline.

We continued this way until the last building. Then, we made a break toward the shoreline as fast as we could. I could see two floaters docked at the edge of the ocean. We ran toward them hoping that no one would spot us at the moment that we were so visible. There was nothing to hide behind and anyone could have seen us.

Our hearts were racing as we came up onto the floaters. Jaye and I jumped into one of them and Denise stood by nervously. She said, "Are you sure you know how to use one of these? They look really high tech." Jaye was already at the back of the floater studying the control panel that was mounted onto the powerful little engine.

The floater had a small wooden area across the middle that was steady for standing on with two benches across. On either side there were big orange floatation devises that ran across the length of the boat. It looked almost like a child's pool toy but with a small engine in the back with controls and lights. I had no idea how to turn it on or make it go forward and I was desperately hoping that Jaye could figure it out.

"It's so simple yet confusing." Jaye said as she began pushing buttons at random. "I take it this is nothing like a Bay Liner." I commented. I tried to study the controls along with her but none of it made sense to me. "What does throttle mean?" I asked. Jaye wasn't listening to me as she continued to try to turn the little engine on.

She must have figured it out because she pushed a button that caused the engine to start. I could feel the vibration in my feet as the little engine revved. I waved to Denise to get in and she did. She looked more nervous than ever but she stood there holding on to my arm as Jaye continued to figure out the controls.

Jaye instructed us to sit down and we did. We sat in the middle of the small boat where there was a bench. It was just big enough for Denise and me to sit closely together. The boat began to move out toward the mainland and away from Clausdrum. Denise began giggling with the thought that we made it. We were prisoners no longer.

Jaye remained focused as she continued to work the controls that she could barely figure out. She pushed another button and we picked up speed. We were heading rather quickly toward the mainland at this point and the prison was looking smaller and smaller as we continued. I began to get excited at the thought that we were free.

Once we were quite a distance from the shoreline, Denise shouted, "We're free! We did it!" Jaye responded, "We're not there yet, Denise." "Oh, come on. We escaped, Jaye." Denise tried to remind her that we had succeeded but Jaye was still far from believing it. I couldn't shake the dreaded feeling that it was too easy. "Denise, we're not out of the woods yet. Jaye is right." I said

Denise sat quietly and celebrated alone. Jaye and I both had a feeling that something could still go wrong. Jaye had sat down across from us and was facing the mainland while Denise and I sat facing toward Clausdrum. As we sat there in silence, I looked up

212

and saw the guards. "I knew it couldn't have been that easy" I said. "They're coming after us." Jaye turned around and saw them as well

It wasn't much of a surprise as we watched them run toward the shoreline and grab the other floater. They looked so small from where we were by this point but they knew how to use the controls of the floater better than we could. Jaye began trying to work the controls once again and this time she was trying to make the boat speed up. We all knew it could go faster since it was a floater but none of us knew how to accomplish this.

Jaye continued to push buttons but the guards had boarded the other floater like trained solders. They were gaining on us rapidly as we struggled to gain speed as well. I walked over to the controls and began trying to push buttons as well. Jaye yelled at me, "Don't touch that! You don't know what you're doing!"

"Neither do you!" I snapped back. As we began to fight over the controls and randomly pushed buttons, the guards were almost as far out into the ocean as we were. By this point, they were approximately twenty feet away. I pushed a button and the boat jerked forward, picking up speed. I stumbled backwards and caught myself but to my horror, I heard a loud splash from the other side of the boat.

I turned back around quickly and saw that Denise was gone. I didn't stop to think about what I was doing before I dove into the icy cold water myself to rescue her. As my body hit the water, pain rushed through every inch of my skin from the coldness of the ocean. The only thing I could think about was rescuing Denise.

She had fallen in and couldn't swim. If I didn't do something to save her, she was going to drown. My whole body was submerged under the ocean waters as I frantically searched the murky water for Denise. I saw no sign of her. Where could she have gone? I knew she couldn't be far since I had jumped in right behind her.

As I continued to search, I knew I would need air soon and planned on coming up to fill my lungs with oxygen and then dive back under. Suddenly, I felt myself being pulled down by the force of the waters. I had gotten caught by a current and I panicked as it pulled me away from the surface. I had no control over my body and I fought with every muscle I had.

The more it pulled and tugged at me, the more my body demanded oxygen. My lungs felt as if they were going to burst as the pain radiated across my entire chest. I couldn't hold my breath any longer. I felt a surge of adrenaline rush through my entire body as my mind knew it was a last resort. With every ounce of strength I had remaining, I pulled myself out of the current that held on to me like the devil's grip.

I rushed up toward the surface as fast as I could to get air. Just as my head broke through the surface of the water, I felt as if I would have passed out with one more second. My lungs quickly filled up with fresh oxygen and my body had a sense of relief that I had never experienced before.

I opened my eyes seconds after taking in the biggest breath of my life and I saw that I was quite a distance from the floaters. No one had seen me from where I was in the ocean at this point. The guards, the floater and Jaye looked small from where I was watching. The current must have carried me further away without me even realizing it.

As I stared back at the scene, I saw Jaye standing to the edge of the floater on one of the orange flotation pieces. The other floater had caught up and was pulled right alongside of the one we had stolen. One of the guards was attempting to board our floater and Jaye was pulling something out of her yellow jumpsuit. I was mortified when I saw that she had a gun.

214

She had stolen one of the guard's guns and hadn't told any of us that she had it. Just as she began to point the gun toward the guard, I heard a loud shot. The sound of it was carried across the water to my ears. To my surprise, it wasn't a Tazer gun that the officer had fired. I watched as I saw blood splatter through Jaye's back. Her lifeless body tumbled backwards into the ocean.

I ducked back down under the water to ensure that I wouldn't be seen. I swam in the direction of the mainland as fast as I could move under the cold waters. By this point, my entire body was numb with the cold. My blood seemed to be moving in slow motion throughout my veins and arteries. I forced myself to continue as I realize that the guards had assumed I had drowned along with Denise.

I swam as close to the surface as I could so that I would avoid the currents below. Now that I knew the currents were there and knew the power they had, I avoided them as much as I could. Each time I came up for another breath of air, I would look back to see where the guards were. They remained out in the middle of the ocean, scanning the waters just beneath them as they searched for our bodies.

I was dead as far as they were concerned but they still needed a body to carry back to the prison as proof that no one had escaped. The Warden would want to believe that his prison remained as a prison that no one could ever escape from. He would have been embarrassed if he had ever known that a prisoner had actually gotten away.

I continued to make progress as I got closer to the mainland. Jaye was dead and Denise had drowned. Kerry had been caught before she was ever free and probably sold us out to the guards. I realized that there was no other way that the guards could have possibility known about the plan unless Kerry had told them.

I wasn't angry with Kerry for saying anything. I figured the guards and the Warden had probably tortured the information out

215

of her. She had been caught at lunch time, which meant that it had taken hours before they had gotten the information from her. Maybe she had waited until that moment before saying anything since she knew that we would be halfway across the ocean by that point.

She had no choice but to give us away since she had to remain behind but she had tried to do us a favor by giving us a head start to freedom. I felt horrible about Denise. She had been worried about drowning and perhaps it was some sort of premonition. We had told her to stay on the boat but she fell off anyway. I smiled when I replayed her last words in my mind.

She died a free woman and that was better than dying as a prisoner. I would have taken death today over living a lifetime in Clausdrum. Even though I hadn't died, I knew that I had been willing for my life to end as opposed to staying in that prison for one more day. Then, I smiled again. But, this time at the realization that I was a free woman.

# Chapter 22
# My Evil Twin

I finally made it to the shallow waters at the edge of the mainland. As the waves crashed over my body, I pulled myself onto the small beach. I was numb from the cold waters and my body was aching. I could hardly pull myself forward let alone stand up. I crawled like a soldier away from the ocean and closer to freedom when I came upon a person standing in front of me.

The first thing I saw was the black boots. As I scanned my eyes upward to see who the boots belonged to, I saw her standing there glaring down at me. It was Sarah Branson. She had come all this way to see me once again. I smiled as I looked back at her and said, "You made it."

She stood there staring back at me, holding the letter I had sent. "I see you made it too." My body suddenly didn't feel as weak anymore as I regained my adrenaline that had kept me going for so long. I pulled myself up and stood in front of her. We were face to face with no glass in between us this time.

"So, you got my letter I see." I had been hoping that she would be in this place at this moment, holding on to that letter. I had sent the letter shortly after she had visited me a few weeks ago to tell her that I was planning on escaping. On the day that she had come to visit me, she had said that she would hunt me down and kill me if I had ever gotten away from Clausdrum. I was counting on that promise she had made when I sent the letter to tell her about my escape plan.

Things could have gone very differently and I knew that as I stared back at her. She could have simply told the police that I was going to escape. I had been nervous over the last couple of weeks that she would take that option. However, she was obsessed with me and I knew that she would rather see me dead than turn me in. I figured she would show up to finish the job when she heard that I was going to be free again.

"You cut your hair." she observed. When she had visited me in prison, I saw how similar we looked as I stared back at her through the glass. We were both the same height. We both had brown eyes. Neither of us was very strong in appearance and both of us were slim built. Both of us had brown hair. The only obvious difference I could see was that my hair was long at that time and hers was cut short.

"Yeah, I did. Now I look a lot like you." I said as I gave her the most sinister smile I could muster up. She realized at that moment what the rest of my plan was. I had intended on stealing her microchip and writing her off as me. I needed to make it look like I didn't survive the escape so that no one would ever come after me.

At that moment, Sarah lunged toward me and grabbed me by the neck. I defended myself and struck back. I pushed her and she stumbled backwards but regained her composure quickly as she came after me again. She wasn't a professional fighter and I could tell right away that she had no idea how to win in a real fight. I had the upper hand and I knew it.

As she tried to get her hands around my neck, I continued to block her arms while I used my leg to knock her off her feet. I swung my leg around and pulled her leg from beneath her and she

218

tumbled. I was over top of her and hit her in the face a few times. She wasn't strong but I realized that she was quick and focused. She swung back and hit me in the jaw.

As we both swung toward each other, she used her entire body to push me off of her. We rolled toward the woods as she gained the upper hand. She was over top of me and before I could stop what was happening, she had her hands around my throat. I could have fought her off but I had another plan.

I let her continue to feel that she was winning as I used my right hand to reach into my jumpsuit without her seeing what I was doing. As she squeeze, she became very confident that she was going to win. As she watched the life going out of my body, she said, "This is for killing my fiancé!" I expected that but I didn't expect what she said next.

"Do you want to know why we were running from you all those years? Wesley didn't kill your sister! I did!" My blood was no longer running cold at this point. I could feel the heat as my blood began to reach its boiling point with anger. I couldn't believe what I had just heard.

"We were running because Wesley thought you were after me! He was trying to protect me. Oh, and you want to know why I killed that little slut? I killed her because Wesley didn't love her. He loved me! She was getting in our way." That was all I needed to hear in order to get one more rush of adrenaline. As I got my hand into my jumpsuit and wrapped my fingers around the scalpel, I could only think of killing Sarah Branson.

I used my thumb to pop the sleeve off of the blade and pulled the knife out. Before Sarah knew what was happening, I had pushed her right arm away from my neck and slid the blade as hard as I could across her throat. She stared back at me in disbelief as blood spewed from her wound. Her other arm went weak as she let go of my throat and clasped her hands around her own neck in a vain attempt to save herself.

219

She fell to the ground and I stood up. I stood over her as she struggled to speak with wide eyes staring back at me. She was gargling and choking as she held on to her neck in a desperate attempt to prevent the blood from leaking out anymore. Blood was soaking into the sand around her body rapidly as the life began to drain from her. I said, "Rot in Hell, bitch!" as I spit on the ground next to her body. Within moments she stopped breathing and her eyes glossed over as they stared back at nothing.

I had won and my plan was complete. I then undressed her body and took off my jumpsuit. I put her clothes on myself and dressed her in the prison uniform I had been wearing. I took the scalpel and found her microchip. I cut along the area and no blood drained out. All of her blood had already drained from her neck. I cut deep into her arm and continued to search her wound until I had the chip in my fingers. I pulled the microchip until it was lose from her arm. Then, I dragged her body to the water's edge.

I held the microchip in my hand and sat back against a tree a few feet away from where her body was lying. I stared back at her lifeless body as the waves crashed up over it. The multiple rushes of adrenaline had caught up with me and my body was exhausted. I knew my plan wasn't over just yet and I had to keep going but I felt that I needed a few moments to rest first. I just sat there staring at the microchip that was now my new identity.

I was now Sarah Branson and had my whole life ahead of me. I thought about all the experiences that had led up to this point and knew that I would have never have guessed that my life would turn out this way. Sarah had money and a nice home. She had opportunities that I never would have had. Sarah had everything and I had nothing.

The tables had turned in that moment as I thought about my new future. I thought about going to college and living my dreams. Dreams I would have never had the opportunity to claim in my past life. Now that I was literally a new person, I could do anything

I wanted. I smiled as I stared back at that small microchip that held my future.

I had to keep moving forward with my plan so I took the scalpel and began cutting the stitches in my arm. I knew it was going to hurt this time even more since I had no Lidocaine to numb the area. I reminded myself that it was something I had to suffer through if I were going to survive. As I continued to cut the stitches away, the wound in my arm reopened and began to bleed a little.

Once the wound was completely open, I shoved the microchip into my arm and tried to keep it from bleeding too much. I took in a deep breath, stood up and faced the wooded area across from the water's edge. I closed my eyes to think about my new future of freedom once again. I reminded myself of my plan and regained the confidence that this would work.

I opened my eyes and took off running as fast as I could through the woods. I was dodging trees and branches as I jumped over logs and kept my feet going as quickly as they would carry me. I came to an opening where there were nice homes just beyond the beach and the woods. I ran to the nearest one as I kept a look of panic on my face. I knocked loudly on the front door.

The door swung open and a man was standing on the other side waiting eagerly for me to tell him what was wrong. A woman came up from behind him along with a small child at his legs. I said in the most convincing way, "I was just attacked and I need help." I showed them my blood stained shirt and wound on my arm and they let me inside immediately. They bought my story. They sat me down and called for an ambulance.

I continued to tell them what had happened. "I traveled here to see a prisoner that is being kept at Clausdrum. She had killed my fiancé about a year ago and I haven't gotten over it yet. My psychiatrist had told me to come here to visit with her for closure and I did. I was planning on going to the prison tomorrow during visiting hours but hadn't decided completely if I wanted to see her or not." They were listening intently as I told my story. I checked their faces and saw that they believed what I had said so far.

I continued, "I arrived at my hotel room earlier today and continued to wrestle with the idea of seeing her tomorrow. After a while of sitting in my hotel room, I couldn't sit there any longer. My anxiety was way too high. I wanted to get some fresh air. I decided to take a cab to where the ferry takes visitors over to the island. I knew the ferry wasn't running but I needed to be close to the prison to think. I wandered along the beach line while I was deep in thought about visiting the prison. I eventually stopped at a quiet location to look out into the ocean. As I stood there, I saw something out in the water and realized there were guards and prisoners fighting on those small boats they have."

The man intervened to explain to me that they are called floaters. I acted as if I didn't already know this as I continued, "Then, while I watched the action from a safe distance, a woman came up onto the shoreline. She had gotten away and swam to the beach. Once she stood up, I saw who it was. It was Roxanne Beatry, the woman who had killed my fiancé."

"Oh, you poor girl!" The woman exclaimed. "What are the odds of that happening?" She was in disbelief at my story but seemed to believe it none the less. They all did as they stared back at me, waiting for me to finish. I showed them my arm where I had cut my own microchip out. Sarah's microchip was hanging out through the wound.

"She had a small knife and she attacked me. I think she was trying to steal my microchip!" I began crying and sobbing as if I had just been through the most traumatizing experience of my life. "I managed to wrestle the knife out of her hands...." I paused to cry some more. "...and I killed her!" I lost it by this point and the woman came over to sit down next to me for comfort.

The ambulance showed up and the paramedics took me to the hospital where a surgeon reinserted the microchip at the bedside. He injected my arm with Lidocaine and I remained awake during the procedure. When he was finished stitching up the wound, he turned to me and said, "It's in there good this time. Nothing can get that microchip out now."

I smiled as I thanked him and a Nurse came in and said, "Sarah Branson?" I replied, "Yes, that's me." "There are some officer's here that just want to ask you some questions." I panicked but reassured myself that I had nothing to hide. I told them the same exact story I had told the innocent family that took me in.

Once I was done telling of the events that had occurred, the officer replied, "That's quite a close encounter you had. You're a very lucky woman, Sarah. The prisoner that attacked you is considered extremely dangerous. She could have easily killed you." I smiled at the irony of the situation.

"We do want to inform you that we have recovered her body. She is no longer a threat to anyone. She's dead." I acted as if I suddenly felt safe again and thanked the officers for bringing me the news about Roxanne Beatry. No one had suspected that I was Roxanne. As far as everyone was concerned, I was Sarah Branson.

I would never be held in a maximum security prison again for the rest of my life. Even though I knew my true identity, I walked out of the hospital, took in a breath of fresh air and lived the rest of my life as a free woman named Sarah Branson. I walked across the street to a small diner, sat down in one of the booths and ordered a steak dinner.

# Chapter 23
# The Recording

**February 12, 2134**

"I never intended to lie to you or anyone else about my true identity. I just wanted a second chance at life. I do hope with all my heart that you will find it in yours to forgive me for this. I couldn't tell you any sooner because I was afraid of being sent back to Clausdrum. You needed to know the truth but I needed to wait until I was long gone from this world before I told you."

The screen went black and the lawyer stood up. He walked over to the recorder and shut it off. He walked back over and sat down on the edge of his desk just waiting for me to say something. I was frozen in disbelief at what I had just watched. There was nothing I could say. I was speechless.

The lawyer finally spoke, "I'm sorry you had to learn about this in such a way. This is the first time I've seen this as well and I can understand that it's a lot to take in." I just turned and looked at him in disbelief. The ground beneath me didn't feel as solid as it had before as I realized that I wasn't who I thought I was. All my life, I had been a descendent of Sarah Branson and now I didn't know anything anymore.

"How long have you known about this?" I asked. "I told you that this is the first time I've seen this recording myself." The lawyer reiterated. I just stared straight ahead toward the large glass window overlooking the city. I still couldn't grasp what I had just seen. "Well, how did you get this recording if you've never seen it before?"

The lawyer stood up and walked over to the large window and explained as he looked out over the busy streets below, "Melissa, your grandmother came to me ten years ago just after she had been diagnosed with Dementia." After all the many years of research and cures for diseases they had found, Dementia still remained the most mysterious disease of all.

In her last days, my grandmother didn't even recognize her own family anymore. I visited every day and was the last to do so by the end. I would sit at her bedside each night after dinner and read to her. She loved books and stories and it comforted her very much. She didn't know who I was but I knew that deep down she loved me and I loved her.

The lawyer continued, "She came into my office one day and handed me this disc. She had made it herself and locked it under a security code that only she knew. That day, she wrote out her Will and left the security code to you. She asked me to hold on to the disc and never let anyone see it prior to her passing. I assumed it was simply a message of her love for her family like most people leave behind on these discs. So, you can imagine that I'm just surprised as you are right now."

"My grandmother wasn't Sarah Branson? She was Roxanne Beatry the whole time and never told any of us?" The lawyer turned back around and said, "It looks that way. She must have made this recording with the knowledge that one day she wouldn't even remember who she was. She wanted you to know the truth, Melissa." "I'm not so sure I wanted to know the truth." I mumbled to myself as the reality was beginning to sink in.

225

My grandmother was Roxanne Beatry, a woman who was charge in the murder of Wesley Strand. She killed Sarah Branson and stole her identity. She had gone to college for interior design and moved to New York City where she met her husband, Daniel Springs. She had gotten married when she was thirty one years old and had two children by the time she was thirty five.

Her children had children, which gave her eight grandchildren by the time she had lost her memories. She was almost ninety years old when she passed away but the Dementia had taken her mind a long time before her passing. She passed away just before her birthday and her gravestone remains with the inscription:

Here Lies Sarah Branson
Mother and Wife
Grandmother
Loved
February 12, 2044 – February 8, 2134
R.I.P.

**About the Author:**

Susan Jones writes thriller/suspense novels and is the author of the Dark Deception trilogy. The first book of the Dark Deception trilogy is called From Her Eyes, which published in 2012. The other two books are The Investigation and The Exorcism, which are both due to publish in 2013. Susan also wrote Clausdrum (Life Without Parole), a crime/suspense novel that published on October 31st, 2012. In addition to writing, Susan is also a Registered Nurse and works full time in a Cardiac Care Unit.

**Other books written by the Author:**

Dark Deception (From Her Eyes)

17375861R00121

Made in the USA
Charleston, SC
08 February 2013